Alice Dippleblack in

Drakoda

By
K. J. Bailey

ISBN: 978-0-9978858-6-6

Chapter 1

It Moved

In the faint orange light of the emberstone cave, Alice asks, "What do you mean it moved?"

The fox girl looks curiously at the large, unhatched egg Danahlia had dropped back among the empty shells of its long gone clutch mates. Kaliska goes for it, but then remembers the two empty ones she put on her hands as gloves and shakes them off before hefting it up to place it against one of her deer like ears. She stands slowly, listening.

"It moved, you know, like the opposite of *not* moving," exclaims Danahlia, the lizard girl looking back between Alice and the egg.

"That is rather difficult to believe," says Twinkaleni, reaching both hands up toward the egg. Kaliska, being much taller than the mouse mage, crouches lower so they can all place their hands about the one whole egg left in the abandoned nest.

"I can feel it, it's alive," marvels Kaliska, brown

eyes wide.

"I don't feel anything," says Alice, her fingers gingerly brushing over the leathery end of the egg.

"Nor I," says Twinkaleni.

"It's in there, but it's weak. We gotta do something," insists Kaliska.

"Like what?" asks Danahlia, tapping a clawed finger on the egg.

Kaliska lets out another goose like honk of a sneeze, then sniffs, giving her head a slight shake, "I don't know."

The girls look to the egg waiting for any hint of life until Alice's stomach reminds her of how long it's been since she'd eaten. She tells the others, "I think the cave is secure enough. Let's go back out, I'm hungry."

Danahlia nods, rubbing her belly, "Yeah, me too."

They decide to collect a generous number of emberstones before heading back to the entrance and place a few of the glowing rocks along the dark tunnel to light the path in case they want more. Kaliska carries what Twinkaleni is certain is a dragon's egg close to her chest, walking hunched protectively over it. As they make their way through once more, they talk excitedly about their discovery.

"You think we can hatch the egg?" asks Alice, reaching out to it but feeling none of the movement Danahlia had described.

"We gotta," insists Kaliska, cradling it with her still dripping robe.

"A Dragon would be nice, but eggs are usually abandoned for a reason. Somethin' might be wrong with it," says Danahlia.

"Wrong with it?" Alice wonders.

"All I know is that in a Liguna clutch, the first eggs to hatch are the strongest and healthiest of the bunch, the late ones tend to be runty, then there's the ones that never make it. I'm not sayin' we shouldn't try, I'm just thinkin' maybe we don't get our hopes too high," explains Danahlia.

This brings a frown to Alice and Kaliska, then Twinkaleni announces, "I, for one, believe we should devote all of our resources to this endeavor."

Attention falls to the smallest of the group and she continues, "A trained dragon would be an enormous asset in our fight against the Order of Thermathrogi."

"Oh no, this dragon isn't for fighting, it's for loving. I can feel it," claims Kaliska.

Alice smiles at the Chitali and asks Twinkaleni, "You know *how* to train a dragon?"

"N-not precisely," replies the mouse girl and Danahlia barks a laugh, earning her a narrow-eyed look while Twinkaleni goes on to say, "But I have studied them in some depth during my time in the Order. Most fascinating creatures, dragons. It is written that their fire can burn anything, even magic."

Alice raises a brow, "Burn magic?"

Twinkaleni nods, "Indeed. To my understanding, dragon fire can unbind the very threads of will that give the spells their shape and form. With such power, even the strongest enchantments the Order can muster will be no obstacle."

"Let's focus on gettin' this guy to hatch before

makin' plans to conquer the world," advises Danahlia.

"How can we hatch it?" asks Alice.

Danahlia, being of cold blood, is the only one of the four who knows much of anything about caring for eggs and says confidently, "First thing is to keep it warm."

"I'll keep it warm," assures Kaliska, hugging the egg even closer.

Danahlia pokes the Chitali in the arm, "You're wet. Alice, you hold it."

Kaliska pulls the egg away to her side as Alice asks, "Why me?"

"Twinkie's too small and I'm not furry. You can keep it warm best for now, here," Danahlia says, handing her the red cloak of the Order she had been wearing. The girls had salvaged the garment off an agent sent to capture or kill Twinkaleni after she had escaped the dreadful institution. Alice puts it on. The cloak was made for someone taller and drags over the ground behind her. She then extends her arms out to Kaliska for the egg. The deer girl purses her lips but relinquishes it.

The egg is quite heavy, perhaps ten pounds, and is as large, if not larger, than the Tokala's own head. She cradles the darkly colored object close, wrapping it in a bit of the cloak while wiping away the moisture Kaliska had left on it. The egg is covered from its tapered end to about two thirds of the way down in smooth overlapping scales. The exposed shell beneath these is rough but slightly pliable. The exact color is difficult to determine but it's very dark, nearly black, even with the scales shimmering in the candle strength emberstone light as they walk.

Alice had dreamed of having a dragon ever since she was a kit and was first told about them by her father. Before the war had claimed him, he had told her of how long ago, dragons were ridden by the great warrior kings who, from the backs of the massive behemoths, defeated the titans that once ruled the land and forged the many kingdoms that then merged into modern-day Arsalia.

Alice ponders the size of the beasts in the stories and then considers the size of the egg in her arms, wondering, "How long does it take for a dragon to reach full size?"

This prompts Twinkaleni to go on in length

about what she has read about dragons. First she says that dragons are believed to be ageless, in that they simply grow larger the older they get. While not truly immortal, as dragons can be slain in battle, they do not die of old age, which means their size is only limited by their years and various environmental factors such as food availability. The small mage continues to say that this, as well as their ability to fly and project great gouts of flame, has made them instrumental in many of Arsalia's greatest conflicts.

Twinkaleni prattles on, "In fact, many noteworthy battles were decided entirely on the dragons that fought in them. The Battle of Blacktide Bay during the second Blood War, for example."

"What happened there?" asks Alice.

Danahlia makes a bored noise as Twinkaleni elaborates. Despite saying she would not go into too much detail, the Murin excitedly gives names of people, places, and background context, including dates, surrounding a battle that took place in the bay of a port city called Twisker. An attempt was made on the city by Cold Blood naval forces intent on blockading the port in order to cut off supplies to embattled Warm Blood armies.

"As the imposing navy began to choke the water way, Wing Commander Theodore Steadhoof led his flight of dragon riders to challenge it. The navy had dragons of their own and both sides watched as the great beasts roared their challenges and dueled over the waters. It's said that their thunderous clash could be heard for miles around and when Steadhoof's dragon riders broke through the enemy lines, the entire naval blockade turned and fled, wooden ships being no match for a dragon's fire. And then, only a matter of months later, the Battle of the Blade Leaf Plains was similarly decided by the two dragon rider champions, Aindrea Ebonclaw and Willard the Valiant, in which..." as Twinkaleni goes on, Alice looks to the egg in her arms, feeling the smooth scales, and thinking she rather likes the sound of Wing Commander Alice Dippleblack.

The Murin mage is forced to cease her history lesson when the party of four nears the cave mouth and the endless crash of water from the falls drowns her out. It's well into night when they wander out along the shore. They continue until they can hear each other once more and consider what to do about food. After the river had supplied them with plenty of fish, Alice, Danahlia, and Twinkaleni hadn't thought to store any and Kaliska, in her haste to return to the trio, hadn't done much foraging.

They're seriously considering joining the still sneezing deer girl in dining on the grasses along the shore of the fall's plunge pool when Alice comes up with an idea.

Setting down the large egg and wrapping it in the crimson cloak, the Tokala takes an arm full of emberstones. The others watch curiously as she tosses them a few feet off shore. Once the glowing stones settle to the bottom, the silhouettes of a few fish coming to investigate can be seen swimming over them. Danahlia grins widely and pushes Twinkaleni forth, pointing enthusiastically. The small Murin bats the larger girl's hands away and walks to the shore where she observes the fishes' movements for a time. Alice and Danahlia watch in eager silence, not wanting to scare the fish away, while Kaliska, a stalwart vegetarian, wanders off with the light of an emberstone to harvest some grass.

When a few fish have gathered around the glow of one of the magic infused stones, Twinkaleni makes her move. Raising both hands high, she calls, "Pavata!" A squat pillar of water rises from the pool and before the fish can escape it, the mouse mage swishes her arms, tossing it ashore. As the water recedes back into the pool, several fish are left flopping in the mud. Alice and Danahlia quickly claim these with a cheer. Then, under guidance of Twinkaleni's light spell, the girls gather sticks and soon have a small fire going.

Exhausted by her uses of magic, Twinkaleni sits by the fire with Kaliska while Alice and Danahlia clean and cook the fish. Kaliska sits with her back to them, now wrapped in their large brown tarp, as she cradles the dragon egg, her wet robe left to dry by the fire. Rather than protest the killing of the fish, Kaliska seems completely absorbed by the egg, watching the firelight dance over its scaled surface.

Once a few fish are cooked, Alice takes two to Twinkaleni and hands one to the small mage. Kaliska doesn't look up, her pink tongue sticking out of the side of her mouth in undivided focus as she stares intently into the egg in her lap.

Twinkaleni accepts the fish with a grateful nod and Alice whispers, "What's she doing?"

The Murin quietly explains, "I believe she is attempting to channel a great deal of her life energy directly into the egg."

Alice's ears angel to the mage, "Life energy? Is that safe?"

Twinkaleni looks to the Chitali, "Not especially, but she believes the dragon may perish if we do nothing."

"What can *we* do?" asks Alice, glancing worriedly at the egg.

Twinkaleni sighs, "There is little we can do but wait." She then begins to nibble on her fish.

Alice frowns and sits down to eat as well. Danahlia joins them silently, a fish in either hand. After a time, she waves one before Kaliska. The deer girl doesn't react at all. Danahlia waves her fish closer, particularly around the Chitali's nose. Alice and Twinkaleni give her irritated looks that only make her smile. When Alice bats away the fish and bares her teeth, Danahlia raises her dinner in surrender and settles to finish eating.

As the girls have their late supper, they watch Kaliska. Gifted with the power of healing, the gold coated deer girl sits with her legs crossed, wrapped loosely in the brown tarp with head held low over the egg. She hasn't moved since she sat down though her eyes are now closed. Danahlia tosses the remains of her fish into the water and stretches, falling back to lay down.

Alice yawns in the middle of picking her teeth with a slender bone and asks Twinkaleni, "Think she's alright?"

The light gray furred mouse girl starts, having dozed off, "Hmm? What?"

Alice grins and gives Kaliska's shoulder a shake, "Hey, Kali." Kaliska silently tips forward.

"Whoa," Alice cries, catching the tall girl by the chest before she can fall over the egg.

"Mmm, mana fatigue. I anticipated this would happen," mumbles Twinkaleni.

Danahlia plucks the egg from the Chitali's lap as Alice carefully lays her down. The brown skinned lizard girl holds up the dragon egg to an ear hole and yawns, "We better get back to the cave. Twinkie, float 'er."

The girls reluctantly get to their feet and gather their things, the Murin mage grumbling, "Asendiote."

With her word, she raises a tiny pink hand and Kaliska lifts limply from the ground. Before it can fall off, Alice catches the tarp and wraps it over the floating girl, holding it in place to preserve the healer's modesty as they shamble back to the cave hidden behind the waterfall.

The acoustics within the cave are such that after a ways in, the constant crash of water muffles to a dull roar. On a fairly open bit of stone the exhausted girls settle down, placing emberstones about themselves. Alice curls around the egg using the red cloak of the Order to hold her body heat and the warmth of their remaining stock of emberstones. Danahlia settles behind her, an arm resting over the Tokala's waist as Kaliska is laid at her back. Twinkaleni uses the slender Chitali's belly as a pillow and they quickly fall asleep.

Alice is awoken when something large slithers over her.

She freezes, her eyes wide but vision blurry, until Danahlia grumbles, "Hey, get off o' me!"

Alice looks to see Kaliska trying to crawl over her.

The deer girl wails, "Where is it? Where is it? Where is it?!" while frantically feeling around the cloak covering Alice.

The fox girl mumbles, "Here," pulling the cloak away to reveal the dragon egg.

Kaliska reaches for it and once assured its safe, she sighs in relief and collapses. Alice and Danahlia wait for a few seconds until a light snoring can be heard from the Chitali. They then roughly push her off and back into place. Twinkaleni grumbles and resettles over the deer girl once more. Alice, feeling the chill of the cave, again drapes the cloak over herself and the egg. Danahlia snuggles her chin into the fur atop Alice's head with a pleased sigh. The Tokala grins, relaxing her head back onto her backpack.

Sometime later, Alice reawakens to Danahlia shifting at her back. The lizard girl stretches and Alice turns toward her. Alice looks into Danahlia's light green, slitted eyes as the Liguna looks back into her sky blue ones.

They smile at each other and touch noses, but then Twinkaleni says from behind Danahlia, "We should begin making preparations to leave this mountain and continue north."

Danahlia turns to the small mage, "Already? What about hatchin' the dragon?"

"We don't know how long that will take and I think it best if we move on quickly," Twinkaleni replies.

Alice stretches and yawns, "Why?"

Twinkaleni sighs, "If word were to get out that dragons have been spotted here, it will attract hunters and trappers from all over. There could be parties already searching as we speak."

"But it's a big mountain, plus everyone thinks it's haunted," reasons Danahlia.

"True, but considering the value of dragons, especially in a time of war, even the supposed specters of the Great Horn will do little to deter such fortune seekers. Worse, if one of the greater houses gets word of dragons nesting here, we may have an entire army on our hands."

This gets the others' attention.

"They'd send an army just for an egg?" Alice asks, rising.

"Especially for an egg," nods Twinkaleni, "An adult dragon would be ill-suited for training and would require tremendous resources to capture, but a newborn dragon would be far easier to manage."

Danahlia reaches over Alice to uncover and lift the dragon egg in their possession, "No way, this one's ours."

Twinkaleni points a tiny pink finger to the egg, "Only as long as we keep it. Which is why I propose we leave and head north toward the Wildlands beyond Arsalia's border."

Agreeing with the Murin, Alice, Danahlia, and Twinkaleni leave the cloak wrapped egg with Kaliska, who hasn't stirred, to begin making preparations for their journey. It's nearly noon when the trio exits the cave and the first thing they do is fish. With Twinkaleni's magic, it doesn't take long at all to get a few over a fire. They take more than they immediately need, wanting to stock a few for their travels. As Twinkaleni lifts balls of water containing fish from the fall's pool and tosses them to shore for Alice and Danahlia to collect, clean, gut, and cook, she readily tells them some history of dragons in Arsalia.

A long time ago, well before the founding of Arsalia, wild dragons roamed all across the land, sea, and sky. Fearsome, long-lived, and able to grow to gargantuan sizes, the behemoths were once worshiped as gods by some early peoples. The fear of living under these great creatures eventually turned to resentment. In time, people learned that not only could dragons be killed by mortal hands but even controlled by them. Those who could kill a dragon were respected, but those who could tame one would come to be revered.

Once controlled, dragons became an instrument of war and the ultimate symbol of power among the budding nations. As techniques were steadily perfected in making them unrivaled killing machines, fear of facing such devastation inspired rivals to tremendous lengths in order to keep enemy dragons from reaching the peaks of their strength. This led to the wide spread sabotage and merciless destruction of training and hatchery programs, which greatly reduced the number of dragons seen in the field. The restless fear of facing enemy dragons was so great that the poaching of wild dragons, along with the destruction and theft of eggs, in a rival's territory was handsomely rewarded. With so much against them for so long, dragons are now commonly believed to be extinct in both Arsalia and Feoria.

Danahlia grins, "They didn't get all of 'em."

Twinkaleni nods, "Indeed. I imagine the

mother of our egg came down from the Wildlands to lay in this mountain, perhaps feeling it safer here."

As they eat their fish, talk turns to how they will feed a baby dragon, should they get their egg to hatch. Alice knows from stories that dragons favor meat but Twinkaleni reveals that they also consume minerals.

"Dragons eat rocks?" asks Alice, munching on a bit of fish.

"Oh yes, mineravore is the correct term. I've read that dragons regularly feed on minerals found in mountains and caves as a means of strengthening their teeth, bones, claws, and even scales. Many wealthy dragon lords are noted for spending exorbitant amounts in order to acquire precious stones for this very purpose."

Danahlia asks with her mouth full, "Har few fayin' veer gonna need tah feed our bragon frubies an' ftuff?"

Twinkaleni stops mid nibble, "Well, perhaps not rubies precisely, but dense minerals would be a worthwhile find if we intend to raise a battle ready dragon."

Danahlia swallows and says with exaggerated enthusiasm, "Good idea, Twinkie. Hey, Alice, remind me to tell Kali to be on the lookout for *diamonds*."

Alice smiles but Twinkaleni huffs, "It was a tremendous bit of fortune that we happened across a dragon's egg. I don't think a few hard rocks will be much more to ask for."

Alice asks, "What about the emberstones? Will they work?"

Twinkaleni nods, "I believe they are a start. The mother dragon laid here because it was the best spot she could find. The emberstones no doubt contributed to this. They not only provided warmth but perhaps also an early source of the minerals a young dragon would need.

"We should get some more then, for the road," suggests Alice.

The others agree and as they're heading back toward the cave they meet Kaliska, finally awoken and heading out with the egg. The deer girl cradles it in both arms with one of her ears pressed to it. She is still wrapped in the tarp and Alice greets her, asking, "How's the egg?"

Kaliska smiles as she passes by them and practically moans, "Warm."

Danahlia and Alice give each other a look as Twinkaleni presses, reaching for the egg, "Well, has your magic had any discernible affect?"

Kaliska lets out a satisfied, "Mmm," and continues on. Unsatisfied, Twinkaleni follows after her with a hail of questions.

Alice is about to follow too, curious about the well-being of the egg, when Danahlia puts a hand on her shoulder, "Guess we're on glowin' rock duty."

The tunnel to the cavern is still lit with the emberstones the girls left behind to mark their passage. Knowing its safe, they walk swiftly to the chamber where they found the dragon's nest. It's dimly illuminated by the muted glow of the magic stones speckling it's surfaces. The pair finds the nest once more, where the emberstones are most concentrated, and briefly rummage through it on the off chance that there might be another unhatched egg. There isn't so they begin gathering emberstones. While the strongest glows emanate from stone still fused to the cavern, there are many loose, smaller ones in a large ring around the dragon egg shells. This makes Alice think the mother dragon must have scraped them from the cave and piled them to help incubate her clutch. Just thinking she is touching stones that were clawed from the mountain by a real live dragon excites Alice and her tail sways as she gathers.

The emberstones are warm to the touch, some of the larger, brighter ones even bordering on hot if held too long with others. Danahlia throws one, sending the glowing rock far into the dark of the cavern. Alice watches as it flies into the distance before hitting something hard, a burst of sparks blooming on impact with a crackling pop. The girls smile at each other over their discovery and Alice hurls an emberstone too. It sails off, bursting into sparks with another fascinating pop. There are plenty of emberstones so they make a game of launching them all over, giving them a scope of just how large the cavern is.

Alice and Danahlia pretend to be mages, hurling fiery bolts at imaginary monsters. They hustle about collecting handfuls of the glowing stones to throw at various rock formations, all while calling out names like "Shatterhead!" and "Chechie!" In the midst of gathering a few more emberstones, Alice feels a slight draft and looks to her left. She finds herself standing before pure darkness. The cave was dark, true, but the specks of light from the emberstones gave it definition, walls, floor, and ceiling. The void before her has nothing, save for the slightest breeze.

The dark unknown and the hint of wind reach for Alice, igniting her curiosity, but at the same time, repelling her. She stands, sniffing the air, perhaps just a fraction fresher than the rotten egg smell of the cavern.

Danahlia joins her and Alice asks, "Where do you think it goes?"

The Liguna points into the gaping blackness, "That way."

Alice gives her a little shove, earning a smirk as Danahlia pitches an emberstone into the new tunnel. It's sent far and doesn't stop until it hits the ground. Alice joins in and they hurl glowing stones all about the passage, giving it some width and depth. They toss some stones upward to find it's considerably taller and wider than their waterfall tunnel. Once they've exhausted their supply of emberstones, Alice has a thought.

"Hey, what if this is the way the mother dragon came in," she says, feeling along the wall and imagining the massive creature digging out the passage with razor sharp claws.

Danahlia agrees, "Yeah, and if that's true, then it must lead out somewhere."

"Maybe through the mountain," suggests Alice, peering into the darkness.

"Would be nice not to have to walk around the entire thing. Let's check it out," says Danahlia stepping forth.

Alice steps back from the foreboding void, "I think we should get Kali and Twinkaleni first."

Danahlia looks back at her, "Huh?" then she grins, "Alice Dippleblack, are you tellin' me you're tuckin'?"

Alice's fur bristles with the insult, "What?! I am *not* tuckin'!"

Danahlia maneuvers around Alice, still grinning while trying to get a look at the fox girl's tail, "You sure? I think you're tuckin'."

Alice backpedals, keeping the lizard girl before her as she throws back, "Am not!"

"Hey, if you're scared, it's fine. We'll go get Mini-Mage and Deernuts to make you feel better," Danahlia teases, trying to reach a hand behind the fox girl.

Alice slaps it away growling, "I'm not tuckin'!"

Danahlia crosses her arms over her chest, waving her own tail over one shoulder, "Really, Alice? After all we been through, you're tuckin' at a little dark?"

"I'm not tuckin' at all, see!" Alice growls, turning to the side to stick out her rump while giving her tail a few waves of its own.

Danahlia concedes, raising both her arms, "Whoa, yeah, look at that. You really aren't tuckin'. Guess you're not afraid at all huh?"

"'Course not," says Alice, looking into the blackness and noting how the few emberstones they've tossed in look unsettlingly like eyes peering back at them.

"Good, good," says Danahlia, pressing another emberstone into her hand, "Then I guess you're leadin,' oh fearless one."

Alice grips the stone, "But…"

Danahlia gives her a questioning look.

Her back against a wall, Alice grits her teeth, "Fine. Let's get more emberstones first."

Danahlia grins and gives a salute, "Yes, ma'am."

Once they've collected a few more hand and pocketfulls, the pair head into the darkness.

Chapter 2

In, Out, and Down

Without Twinkaleni to use her magic, the faint glow of the emberstones are all that light their way. With the strength of a single candle, their fistfuls of glowing rocks do little to illuminate the large tunnel and the two occasionally flick some forward and around to get an idea of what lies before them. Cautiously slow, Alice walks with tentative, sweeping steps to avoid stubbing a toe, though so far the tunnel seems fairly clear of debris. Danahlia moves similarly with her lengthy tail held before her feet. Getting little use from their eyes, the girls listen, Alice's ears angling around at every sound, but these only emanate from the girls themselves.

The large tunnel takes a subtle turn and begins to ascend ever so slightly. Alice and Danahlia continue to follow it, tossing emberstone pebbles about. They occasionally toss a stone high up. Doing so let's them see that the tunnel remains fairly uniform throughout, staying several times their height. This leads them to suspect that the dragon that dug this burrow must have been massive. Then Alice has an unsettling thought.

"You don't think other dragons might wanna

use this cave to lay their eggs, right?" she asks.

Danahlia hesitates for a moment, "N-nah, no way. That we even got to see some old eggs is practically unheard of nowadays. No way we'd see a full grown dragon. Not on this one mountain, in this one cave, no way," the lizard girl continues, shaking her head, "No chance, not one, mm-mm."

It's hardly convincing, but the pair move on anyway, neither willing to let the other consider them a tucker.

After a fairly short time, Alice is holding the last few of her emberstones while wondering how to broach the subject of going back without having her courage questioned. She tosses one forth and follows its route only to have it abruptly vanish. Before she can even guess at why, her nose blooms in pain when she walks face first into a wall. The Tokala yips, jerking back while raising a hand to her throbbing nose and front teeth.

Danahlia bursts with a laugh, "Bfha! How'd that rock taste?"

Alice glares at her companion and kicks her in the shin.

"Ah!" Danahlia cries, backing away, "Hey!"

Alice tries to check if she's bleeding but in the dim light she can't tell.

Danahlia approaches and tries to get in front of her, "Does it hurt?"

"Yeah it hurts!" Alice throws back at the idiotic question, turning away.

Danahlia holds her by the shoulder, "Come on, lemme see."

Alice grudgingly lowers her hand and lets the taller girl take a look. Danahlia holds an emberstone between them as she tries to see by its faint light. Alice watches the Liguna bob before her, trying to get a better angle to examine her injury by. Their eyes meet and Danahlia grins just before giving Alice's nose a little lick. Alice turns away and gingerly wipes her nose on a sleeve, mostly to hide her own smile.

Danahlia says thoughtfully, "Doesn't taste like blood."

Alice's nose still throbs but confident at least that it isn't bleeding, the two crouch to relocate the disappearing emberstone. It turns out to have rolled into another tunnel, this one much smaller than the one they stood in, only coming up to about mid-thigh. It's roughly rounded and about as wide as it is tall. The emberstone Alice tossed sits maybe a foot inside. The pair peer into the darkness beyond the glowing rock and listen, hearing nothing.

"Wonder who made this," ponders Alice aloud, her voice echoing across the fairly smooth walls.

Danahlia stands, "Don't know," then, rolling around a remaining few glowing pebbles in her palm, says, "Hey, we're runnin' outta light. Let's think about headin' back."

Alice grins widely, victory in sight, "Danahlia Smoothide, are you startin' to tuck?"

Danahlia steps back, her eyes widening, "No! Course not. I'm sayin' we need light for *your* safety," she points accusingly at Alice, then smirks, "'Less you like kissin' rocks."

Alice narrows her eyes at the Liguna for a second, then swiftly turns and starts deeper into the main tunnel with forced confidence.

"Hey, come on. We can't keep goin' in the

dark, it's dangerous," warns Danahlia.

Alice calls over her shoulder, "You can tuck tail and run if you want to, but I wanna see where this goes."

Danahlia stays put, "Come on, Alice. This is *me* sayin' it's dangerous. Let's go back."

Alice ignores her, instead placing one hand on the wall while holding out her other, the last of the emberstones barely illuminating her own palm as she presses on.

"Fine, I'm goin' back. Don't blame me if you get lost," says Danahlia, and Alice can hear the lizard girl's toe talons rapping against the stone floor as she takes a few steps in the opposite direction. She calls again, "Probably gonna end up cave monster food."

Alice continues undeterred.

After a few moments she hears the Liguna's grumbling echo, "Ticks!" and then her toe talons rapping rapidly back toward her. When Danahlia catches up, she states, "If we die in here, my ghost is gonna haunt yours good."

Alice just smiles.

The pair moves even more cautiously, keeping an emberstone each held before them. As they wander on, Alice considers if she made the right decision. So far, the only indication that this tunnel led anywhere positive is the slightly lowered rotten egg smell. The air is damper here as well and accompanied by the lightest breath of a breeze. Alice can also hear, very occasionally even feeling, dripping water. They're making their way around another turn and Alice is planning to tell Danahlia she's ready to head back when the fox girl spots a small, faint, green glow a little higher than eye level.

"Hey, what's that?" she asks pointing, making her way toward it.

Danahlia tugs on her tail before she can get much closer, "Hold on, that might be alive."

The two observe it for a moment but it doesn't move. Danahlia's emberstone dips down as she rummages around on the ground, coming up with a pebble. She tosses it underhand at the glow but in the near absolute darkness, it's impossible to see if she hit anywhere near it. Alice waves her emberstone around to get some sort of response from the glow but it does nothing. After a few more pebbles are tossed, the girls approach.

On closer inspection, the glow turns out to be emanating from a blotch of some sort of algae growing on the cave wall. Alice feels over it, finding it damp and somewhat squishy while smelling of wet soil.

"Well, congratulations, Ms. Dippleblack. You've discovered some fine glowin' slime," says Danahlia, making a trail through it with a claw. Alice scrapes some up and smears it on one of Danahlia's forearms, "Ugh! Hey!" the Liguna cries, but then seeing the algae on her arm retains its glow, she says with new interest, "Hey."

"Wags," Alice grins and looks down the tunnel to see more.

They venture forth, their caution quickly turning to curiosity. The further they go, the more glowing algae coats the walls, ceiling, and floors. It starts out as splotches here and there, then larger patches, and soon much of the cave's surfaces are covered. They glow in different colors, most green, but some blue, brown, and even pink. A few of these have wavy lines going through them as if someone passing by had scrapped the algae off with a finger, leaving trails of black through fields of multicolored glow. The pair investigates these trails to find they all end with strange round rocks. In the dim light, they appear black as the rest of the cave but shift a little when touched, like a loose tooth. Alice pries one up and rolls it around in her hand.

It isn't perfectly round and on the underside there's a bit of algae stuck to it. As Alice inspects the rock, she notices the glow on the bottom pulsate. As she watches, the pulsating glow grows, widening before her eyes.

Alice bats at Danahlia, who's begun spreading more algae on her arm, using a claw to make intricate patterns on her skin, "Hey, look at this."

"Oh, they're snails. Guess they eat this stuff. Must make 'em glow too," says the Liguna.

Alice's imagination must have gotten away from her because as she rolls it in her palm a bit more, she recognizes it.

She then places the snail back on its trail and Danahlia asks, "You ready to head back yet?"

Alice looks deeper into the tunnel, the glow of the algae showing that it curves again further ahead, "Shouldn't we see if this tunnel actually leads out?"

Danahlia wipes her finger along the bridge of Alice's muzzle, leaving a moist, glowing streak, "It has to. Where else would it go? Besides, we shouldn't leave Twinkie and Kali alone too long. Who knows what might get 'em if we're not around."

Alice concedes and the two begin heading back the way they'd come. As they return to the emberstone cavern, they spot a familiar orange light and call to Twinkaleni. The tiny mouse mage joins them, irritated that they'd been gone so long.

"Sorry, but we found this tunnel and thought it might lead out to another part of the mountain," explains Alice.

The mouse mage looks past them, her short arms crossed over her chest in a pout, "And does it?"

Danahlia shrugs, "Don't know, it's pretty long. Where's Kali?"

Twinkaleni informs them that Kaliska managed to succumb once more to mana fatigue after channeling her own life energy into the dragon egg in an effort to give it the strength needed to hatch. The trio returns to their camp to retrieve their supplies and the sleeping Chitali. On the way, Alice and Danahlia tell Twinkaleni about the new tunnel and the Murin agrees that it is worth investigating. Heading back to the algae tunnel, the girls are sure to gather more emberstones. Twinkaleni uses her magic to not only create a light but also to hold Kaliska afloat with her gravity altering earth magic. Alice offers to carry the deer girl for a while but Twinkaleni insists on doing it herself, saying its good practice.

Ever impressed with the mouse mage's growing powers, Alice trails just behind Kaliska, who appears to be sleeping soundly on a mattress of air. Alice guides the Chitali some with a hoof, to keep her from spinning or bumping into walls. Kaliska's hooves are cloven, black, and hard, but very small. Alice toys with them, wondering how anyone could walk on such dainty feet, her own bare paws being considerably larger.

Twinkaleni is fascinated with the glowing algae, saying it has no magic but glows due to some "bioluminescence." The ball of light she holds high in the air borrows the algae's glow, causing the algae to dim while her light changes colors to match it. It's eerily beautiful to watch the glow vanish only to have it charge and change Twinkaleni's magical light.

Further along the tunnel, the patches of algae are steadily becoming unavoidable. There are more snails here as well, big ones. Some of them have shells nearly a foot in diameter. There's more moisture too, making the slimy algae rather slippery under foot. The party does their best to press forward but eventually they come to an incline that they simply can't manage with all the algae. It's not terribly steep or even all that long but with the floor of the tunnel so slippery, even Danahlia's taloned feet have trouble getting any traction.

After she slides down for the sixth time, the lizard girl negligently slings the algae from her hands, "Well, now what?"

Twinkaleni informs them of what they already know, "My magic could get you all to the top, but-"

"You can't fly yourself up there," Alice finishes, frowning.

Twinkaleni nods, "Indeed, but perhaps you can find something, vines, perhaps roots or some such."

"Nah, we aren't leavin' ya here alone," says Danahlia, looking about for some alternative route.

The girls have passed multiple smaller tunnels similar to the one Alice had lost an emberstone in and the Liguna offers, "Maybe one o' those other tunnels leads up there."

"Possible, but it would take a great deal of time to inspect each one and we don't have enough food or water to remain within this mountain for long."

"Besides, who knows what's in those tunnels," adds Alice.

Looking over the clear patches the group had made through the algae with their attempts to scale the slope, Alice has an idea, "Hey, maybe we can use the snails."

"To clear the algae? That would take some time. Snails are not known for their speed," says Twinkaleni.

"But if we get a whole bunch of 'em," Alice reasons.

Then Danahlia finishes, "Yeah, maybe they can clear enough."

Twinkaleni shrugs, "I suppose it is worth a try."

The trio gather as many snails from along the tunnel as they can, favoring the largest. They place them on the impeding algae where they can reach, mostly near the base of the slope, though Twinkaleni uses her magic to place many along a narrow path up it. Then they wait, exhausted from the effort.

There is no way to know what time it is but they guess it must be late in the evening or even night already. The girls do what they can to clear a space and lay out their tarp so they don't have to sleep on the damp cave floor. Kaliska wakes while they're eating from their store of fish and immediately takes a liking to the snails. She watches, enraptured, as they "race" across the algae. She keeps the dragon egg in her lap, hunched over it protectively while telling the others of it's improving condition.

As the girls settle in, Alice paints some more algae over Danahlia, the glow showing far better on her smooth skin. She makes a few flower-like designs along the Liguna's arm with a few spots over them, one green and one blue. She says these are Tally and Shae, their pixie friends from the forest near Alice's hometown. Danahlia smiles wearily, more interested in looking at Alice than her work.

Twinkaleni had fallen asleep shortly after eating and, with Kaliska on watch, the pair decide to follow suit.

Sometime later, Alice's eyes flash open when she hears Kaliska scream, "Stop! Ricky, no!"

Through bleary vision, Alice looks around in alarm, feeling Danahlia shifting at her back.

"What? What's goin' on," the Tokala demands.

"Guys, help! They got Ricky and the others!" Kaliska wails, trying to scale the slope while pointing frantically up it.

Alice pans her gaze along the algae covered incline to several large, dark blotches among the various glows. At first she thinks these are just areas cleared by the snails but then she notices them moving.

"What are those?" asks Danahlia, moving to retrieve her boar spear.

Twinkaleni calls, "Estraleete!" summoning a ball of bright greenish light that causes the glows from the party's emberstones and the tunnel's algae to dim.

The mage sends this up to the moving blotches and in the light, the girls can make out dark furred bodies with large, thickly clawed limbs. The light seems to startle the creatures and they scatter before it, retreating into the smaller tunnels along the sides of the main one. As the last is fleeing, Alice makes out a pair of beady eyes and what might be a pink nose, though it looked to have short fleshy fingers sprouting in a ring around it.

Before Alice can draw her sword, the creatures are gone and the cave is silent once more, save for Kaliska's defeated cries. Alice and Danahlia hold their weapons and peer around the cavern, listening and watching while Twinkaleni illuminates the area. Nothing stirs.

Once they're sure they're alone, Alice asks the weeping Chitali, "Are you ok? What were those things?"

"I don't know. They came out of the tunnels. They seemed friendly but then they started taking 'em," Kaliska whimpers.

"Taking who?" asks Twinkaleni, letting her light go out, the glow of the algae and emberstones returning when she does.

"Charlie, Tipper, Jonesy, and they even got Ricky. I could only save Silvester," Kaliska cries, showing them the medium sized snail cradled in her hands.

"You, they took the snails? You *named* the snails?" asks Danahlia.

Kaliska nods, her lower lip quivering as she looks down at the one she's holding, hiding in it's shell.

Looking up the slope and waiting for her heart to slow, Alice sees that the snails had done a fair job of clearing out some spots, perhaps the furred creatures doing a part as well. There are still more than a few snails left, though it appears the creatures have taken the largest of them.

"Aww, they took all the big ones. I wanted those," Danahlia whines.

Kaliska gives her a dirty look while gently stroking her snail's shell. Twinkaleni and Alice inspect the snails' trails through the algae to find that they are quite sticky.

"Maybe we can use this," suggests Alice,

pulling her hand off a trail and feeling it tug her fur.

Twinkaleni nods, "Yes, but we should act quickly. Who knows how long we have before this substance dries."

The mouse mage doesn't have the reach to manage so Danahlia carries the diminutive Murin on her back and makes the climb with her. Alice notices Kaliska hasn't made any move to progress and begins getting her things together, namely putting the dragon egg back in her basket along with the emberstones to keep it warm. As she does, she tries to console the distraught Chitali.

"Sorry some of the snails got taken, Kali," says Alice, "But think about it, there are lots more snails in the tunnel and those few that got taken are probably feeding those creatures' babies or something." Kaliska just sighs so Alice goes on, "And you know, if they didn't eat some of the snails, there might not be enough algae to go around, which means the snails would starve and die anyway. This way only a few are taken and the rest get to live. Plus, the few that get taken means those ferals get to live too. That's good, right?"

Kaliska looks over to her but before she can say anything, Danahlia calls down, "Hey! Quit scratchin' your fleas and hurry it up! I think we're almost outta here!"

Alice smiles at the Chitali, putting a hand on her shoulder, "You ready to go?"

Kaliska looks down at her snail and then back up the slope before setting it on a bed of algae, "Bye, Silvester. Try not to get eaten. Grow so big they won't even want to mess with you."

She then accepts her basket and the two begin the climb.

Twinkaleni holds the light for them as they slowly make their way up. It's messy work since there's still slimy algae over their path and they have to lay their forearms and shins flat against the rock to get the most traction out of the sticky snail trails, but they manage. When she reaches the top Alice expects to see the light at the end of the tunnel from what Danahlia said, but instead it just looks like it goes on.

Danahlia seems to sense Alice's unasked question, saying, "Smell that? Air's fresher here. This tunnel has to end soon."

All Alice can smell is the heavy, damp soil scent

of the algae all over the front of her clothes and fur.

Then Twinkaleni points out, "Possible. Equally possible is that the air is venting through one of the smaller tunnels."

"I choose to hope," Danahlia grins.

The girls do their best to wipe themselves off and continue down the main tunnel. They peer into each of the smaller tunnels they pass, sniffing and checking for any sign of daylight or fresh air. After a time of finding none, the still weary party decides to take a break. They lay out their tarp once more, being sure to place the algae covered side down and have some water.

Kaliska watches more snails while Alice and Danahlia lay beside each other, but after the excitement of the creatures and climbing the slope, they find it difficult to go back to sleep. They watch Twinkaleni sitting nearby, making loose fingered gestures at the air all around her as if trying to collect it into an invisible bubble. Within a few minutes, they can see small drops of water forming where the little mouse girl directs the air. She stops once she has a small ball the size of her own tiny fist floating before her. The ball divides into four smaller drops and they drift off to hover before each of the girls who all stick their tongues out to lap them up.

Twinkaleni's water is warm but sweet, tasting cleaner and fresher than any they could gather from a stream or pond. She had said that this was likely due to any remnants of dirt and other contaminates being left behind when she pulled free the fine particles of water vapor. The Murin mage lets out a pleased sigh and rolls to her back as her companions praise her efforts. She quickly falls asleep and by the dim glow of the algae, so do they.

After a brief respite, the girls continue on and eventually reach daylight. It's blinding after being in the dark so long and they take a moment to let their eyes adjust. From the sun pouring into the cave, they can see that it's late in the morning. More, they've come out somewhere on the eastern side of the Great Horn.

Kaliska rushes out to greet the day with open arms, cheering. The others follow close behind, eager to be free of the cave's damp darkness. The sun welcomes them with gentle warmth and Alice lets her backpack slide from her arms to embrace it. She closes her eyes to the brightness and lets the morning take the moisture from her fur and clothes.

"Ahh! Finally," exclaims Danahlia, stretching

out, her tail pointing straight back and poking Twinkaleni.

The light gray furred Murin pushes it aside, looking pleased that they've finally left the cave. "This is excellent," she says happily, "We've no doubt shaved days from our trek going through the mountain rather than around it."

"Yay!" Kaliska cheers jubilantly and begins spinning with her arms out.

Alice grins, watching the Chitali from the corner of her eye as she takes in the sun. Then she notices something off about the landscape near the deer girl's feet and realizes they're on a cliff.

"Kali!" Alice shouts, reaching out as the Chitali obliviously spins closer and closer to the edge. Alice manages to grasp the deer girl by a hand and pulls her away from the cliffside, although Kaliska seems to think that the Tokala just wants to join her and the Chitali starts spinning with Alice, giggling. Alice manages to guide them further back before letting Kaliska go, the deer girl spinning dizzily into Danahlia.

"Ticks that was close," says the Liguna, shoving Kaliska lightly away so she can look over the edge.

"You have to be more careful, Kali," admonishes Alice peering down the cliff as well.

They aren't immensely high, but the fall of several stories would still be disastrous. Looking around, Alice finds that they're standing on some sort of plateau right before the cave mouth with only a sliver of a trail leading to the north along a sheer rocky cliff that looms over them.

"Huh? Wha- Oh," bubbles Kaliska, as her attention is taken by some roosting birds that have made their nests on outcroppings protruding from the cliffs above and below them.

From what the fox girl can see, they look to be birds of prey, shaped and colored similarly to eagles with impressively large bodies and short curved beaks. There is a single bird in each nest watching Alice's party warily and silently.

Twinkaleni is looking around at the cliff they stand on and gushes in a rare moment of excitement, "Just think. At some point, a great mother dragon chose this very spot and began digging the cave which we have just traversed."

"Yeah, fascinating," says Danahlia passingly as

she watches Kaliska approach the large birds, "Hey Kali, maybe not bug 'em, huh?"

"Kali, don't. They're probably gonna get mean if you get too close to their nests," adds Alice.

Without looking back, Kaliska calls, "I'm not gonna bother 'em, I just wanna see-"

The nearest of the birds lets out a sharp shriek and flaps its wings threateningly at the Chitali. Kaliska jumps back as the others birds make similar noises to show their irritation at the party's intrusion. The deer girl frowns at the birds as she quickly makes her way back to the others, the avians glaring after her.

Danahlia grins at this, "Well, we can try to climb down or try to get through those birds."

"Perhaps they will go in search of food soon," offers Twinkaleni, observing them from a safe distance.

"Nah, betcha they're all sittin' on eggs. They won't leave 'em," the Liguna informs.

"We could take a few, scare off the rest, maybe even get some eggs out of it," suggests Alice.

Kaliska is quick to shoot this down, "No! You can't, especially if they have babies!"

Danahlia sighs, "Well, what then? You wanna try to climb down this sheer cliff face and hope those things don't take advantage?"

Kaliska tentatively steps to the edge to look down at a decent of perhaps twelve meters, then nods, "We can do it."

"I could levitate you all down there," offers Twinkaleni.

"Yeah, then we could catch you in the tarp," adds Alice.

Danahlia and Kaliska agree to this though Twinkaleni doesn't seem as enthusiastic.

Alice is the first to be lowered to the rocky ground below. Twinkaleni's magic transfers Alice's own weight elsewhere, making the fox girl incredibly light. She doesn't float off in the wind but it's enough to let her descend the forty or so feet to a comfortable landing. When she hits the ground, her slim build's weight is restored and she looks around to the nearby trees and shrubs. Seeing nothing threatening, she calls up to her friends. Danahlia descends next. Then Kaliska.

As the Chitali is floating down, Alice notices the roosting birds shifting about, taking great interest in the party's movements. Kaliska is about two thirds of the way down when the birds make their move. Perhaps the party of four together was too daunting, because once the Murin mage is alone the large birds begin to leave their nests with powerful flaps of their wings.

"Twinkaleni, look out! The birds!" Alice shouts as Danahlia tries to pull the bow over her shoulder free. The Liguna manages to get it but before she can nock one of their three remaining arrows, Kaliska's scream takes their attention. The deer girl falls, flailing wildly, as Twinkaleni loses hold over her spell, turning to confront the encroaching birds. Danahlia only has time to turn before the tallest of the group crashes into her from above. She clips Alice as well, taking them all to the ground.

Alice bumps her head on something hard. As the world spins nauseatingly around, she feels the others wiggling beside her. On the cliff, she spots the birds gathering and a stream of fire flies into one. The struck bird screeches in panic and flies off with a trail of smoke, but the others persist. Alice sees several more streams of fire emerge though its clear the small mage is firing out of desperation. Alice forces herself to her feet, the blood rush making her vision uncertain.

Without knowing if she can but knowing Twinkaleni may perish if she doesn't try, she shouts up to the Murin, "Jump! I'll catch you!"

The Tokala alertly scans the cliff's edge for any sign of the tiny girl so she might position herself under her. After another beam of fire lashes out at the birds, Alice sees Twinkaleni throw herself off the edge of the cliff. Alice immediately angles herself to catch, arms spread wide, but to her horror one of the birds grabs the tiny Murin by a leg in its long, viciously curved talons. Even twice and more the size of the mouse girl, the bird has trouble staying aloft with its catch and is quickly attacked by the others. As it attempts to defend itself, Twinkaleni is let go, only to be grabbed again by another one of the birds. Alice watches helplessly as the mouse girl is juggled from one bird to another under a hail of talons and angry piercing cries.

"Get off o' me!" Danahlia shouts, taking Alice's attention.

The Liguna is trying to pry Kaliska off, the

Chitali hugging her ferociously while thanking her over and over for breaking her fall. Then Alice remembers the bow and takes it up along with one of their last arrows. Her eyes zip up and down as she nocks the arrow while trying to keep watch of Twinkaleni. Alice draws, sights the bird clutching her dangling friend, and lets loose. The bird comes under attack and narrowly evades the shot, freeing Twinklaleni to drop again. The arrow strikes, instead, the attacking bird as a third goes for the falling Murin. Each time she's dropped, Twinkaleni makes it a few more precious feet to the ground and to the safety of her friends.

Alice feels something wet and warm drip onto her face but she ignores it, quickly nocking another arrow and loosing it into the offending birds.

Over there squawking she can hear Danahlia shouting, "HEY! Get away from her!" as the Liguna hurls a few stones.

Kaliska joins in and once Alice fires her last arrow, scoring another hit, the birds give up with angry shrieks. Twinkaleni limply falls the last few yards into Danahlia's arms. She's covered in blood.

Chapter 3

Down The Great Horn

"Twinkie? Twinkie? Come on, say somethin'," begs Danahlia, cradling the silent Murin.

Alice and Kaliska quickly approach, Alice glancing back up to see the surviving birds grudgingly returning to their nests.

"Oh ticks, there's so much," cries Danahlia, trying to pull away some of the mouse girl's bloody, shredded garments to find her wounds. One of the Murin's great ears has a ragged slice running from the bottom up nearly a third of the way.

"Oh no," Alice whimpers, dropping her bow.

"Kali, help her!" demands Danahlia.

"Uh, uh, ok, I'll try," Kaliska says tentatively, putting her hands on the small, still form. She tries to take her from Danahlia but the Liguna only holds tighter. "I need to see where she's hurt," says the Chitali, making a greater effort to extract the Murin from the Liguna's grasp.

"Everywhere, just heal 'er!" Danahlia shouts,

tears welling in her eyes.

"I have ta see!" Kaliska insists.

Alice puts what she hopes is a comforting hand on Danahlia's arm and Twinkaleni's tattered, bloody shirt, "Come on, Danny, let's set her down so we can figure out how to help her."

The lizard girl glares back murderously for a second but then concedes to gently lay the small girl on the thickest bit of grass she can immediately find under the shade of a tree. They all crouch around as Kaliska slowly pulls up Twinkaleni's shirt. The blood makes the fabric stick to her fur a bit before revealing a terrible puncture near her navel. Alice takes in a breath through clenched teeth, but this is only the first of many.

They remove the tiny Murin's oversized clothes to reveal that she is covered with slashes and stabs from the cruel talons of the awful birds. Crimson mats her usually light gray fur into patchworks of reds and pinks forcing Kaliska to prod around to find the more severe wounds. All Alice can think is how someone so small could have so much blood.

"Is... is she alive?" she asks nervously.

"Course she is," Danahlia growls without looking up, then sniffs, "Few birds aren't enough to bring down Twinkie. We been through plenty worse, *plenty* worse."

Kaliska says nothing. Instead she begins to prioritize wounds, healing the deep punctures around the Murin's torso first. After she manages to seal a few, the Chitali breathlessly tells the girls to get her basket and tear up clothes for bandages. Alice retrieves the large basket Kaliska generally carries on her back from where it fell and notices the dragon egg has tumbled out. She takes only a second to look around but doesn't see it, though she finds a stash of leaves smooshed at the bottom of the basket. She brings these to Kaliska who wearily selects a few, then just before toppling over says, "Chew…"

"What? Kali, what?" Alice asks, shaking the Chitali's shoulder but finding she's out cold.

Danahlia, tearing her own shirt into strips, asks, "What she say?"

"Uh, I think she wants us to chew these leaves and put them on the wounds," says Alice, regretting not listening more carefully all those times Kaliska rambled on about the healing properties of various plants.

They do, finding the leaves terribly bitter and sour. Once pulped, they spread some carefully over each wound and do their best to tie bandages over them. Even so, there aren't enough of the leaves to coat all so Alice heads off to find more among the forest of the Great Horn's eastern slope.

Alice searches frantically, eyes panning over bushes for the right shaped leaves. When she spots some that look right, she breaks them in half and tastes them to make sure they have the same terrible flavor. Once she finds the proper plant, she strips it of its healing leaves and dashes back to Danahlia. She finds the Liguna still sitting beside the unconscious pair, having adjusted their positions to make them more comfortable.

With the new leaves pulped, they manage to cover the rest of the small mouse girl's wounds. Looking over Twinkaleni, lying motionless and badly hurt, brings back memories of Lyca and the forest children. Alice shakes her head furiously, trying to keep the thoughts from taking hold. Deciding it's best to distract herself, the young fox girl starts to gather the party's scattered belongings. She places everything against the trunk of a tree and then decides to go look for their missing dragon egg.

Danahlia hasn't moved an inch since setting Twinkaleni down.

Alice finds the egg easily enough among some thick grass. It's rolled quite a ways but looks intact. Picking it up, she finds it feels heavier than the last time she held it and either the color has changed or she's just noticing that it's not actually black, rather it's a very deep red. The Tokala then places her cheek against the leathery end below the scales. The sun has kept it warm making it feel rather pleasant against her fur. Alice holds the egg for a little while, letting the warmth sooth her troubled mind. The egg shifts. She pulls away, looking at it in surprise. It was just a subtle movement but it definitely came from within, as if the baby dragon pushed against the shell from the inside. Alice places it against her cheek again, eyes wide in wonder. The egg shifts some more. Alice's tail wags a bit as she hurries back to Danahlia.

"Hey Danny, the egg, it's movin'. I think it might hatch soon," says Alice, holding the dragon egg in both hands.

Danahlia glances over to her with a forced half grin, "That's good."

Alice frowns and places the egg in the sun to

keep warm while crawling over to Twinkaleni, "She any better?"

Danahlia takes in a deep breath, slowly letting it out, "I don't know, maybe."

Alice wedges herself in between Twinkaleni and Danahlia, placing an ear to the Murin mage's mouth. The sensitive white fluff in her ear is tickled by the faintest breath. Alice lets out a relieved sigh and looks up to the Liguna, "She's breathing."

"'Course she is. What I tell ya? Few birds aren't near enough to take Twinkie down," Danahlia says with a sniff, a wide smile spreading over her face.

She fiddles with Alice's ears, making them twitch, until the Tokala moves. Alice then busies herself by laying out the large brown tarp along with some of the group's clothes so the sun can dry the algae on them. Once she's done, Alice spots the two birds she'd managed to hit with arrows and goes to retrieve them. One is still alive, though seems to have been crippled by the fall to the rocky ground. Its head moves a little, an eye watching Alice, though its body is completely still. A broken arrow shaft pokes out from under its breast. The Tokala hurries to get her sword and ends the beast by taking off its head. She does the same for the other so the blood can drain. Looking up, she sees the others sitting in their nests, some watching her drag away the bodies of their kin.

Under the relative safety of their tree and beside Danahlia, Alice is free to examine the birds. They are very large with impressive wing spans. She plucks a few of their long, gray and black feathers, thinking they would make good fletching for arrows. Their thick talons are long, sharp, hooked, and black, four on each fire colored foot. Some are bloodied, prompting Alice to look over to Twinkaleni and hope Kaliska can heal the damage they had done.

As Alice continues pulling out feathers, setting aside some for arrows, Danahlia eventually joins her, plucking the other bird. Alice had gotten used to hunting and preparing animals for food. She didn't particularly like it, especially the messy parts, but found that if she worked quickly and didn't think on it too hard, it really didn't bother her much anymore.

The pair discuss moving to a safer place, away from the large birds and their nests, but aren't sure if moving Twinkaleni in her condition would be a good idea. Alice brings up their diminishing water supply and volunteers to scout the area later for water and shelter, knowing Danahlia would much prefer to stand guard over Twinkaleni. She then decides to look around for fire wood so they can cook their nearly feather free birds.

The dense forest has more than a few pine trees shedding their highly flammable needles in preparation for the coming winter and Alice gathers them up along with fallen branches. As the sun slowly descends, her ears pick up the calls of unfamiliar ferals and she quickly finds her way back to Danahlia. The Liguna is cleaning out one of the birds and uses a knife to cut it into more manageable hunks so Alice gets a fire going with her flint and steel.

Its evening and the pair are sitting beside the fire cooking the bird meat directly on the flames. The scent of warm food is permeating the air when Kaliska startles them, suddenly taking in a sharp inhale while rising to a sitting position. She immediately tends to Twinkaleni, asking for water and food while gently prodding around the Murin's heavily bandaged form. Danahlia hands her some water, but they hadn't thought to gather any greens and Alice runs off to look for the sort Kaliska generally ate.

It's not hard to find food for her, a benefit of

eating almost anything green Alice figures as she gathers a few pocket fulls. By the time she gets back, Kaliska has passed out again. Danahlia says she healed Twinkaleni a little before succumbing to mana fatigue once more.

"Did she say anything else? Did she say how Twinkaleni was doing? If she'll live?" Alice asks, piling the gathered greens beside the Chitali for when she wakes up.

"Naw, she just rubbed Twinkie's legs and arms for a minute, then dropped. But I think that means she's doin' better, because she was healin' her arms and legs, not her chest. That's where all the important bits are, ya'know?" says Danahlia, gently stroking their smallest companion's forehead.

Alice hopes this is the case and the pair eats while they watch over their friends.

Alice is awoken by Danahlia that night to take her turn on watch. Alice groggily gets to a sitting position while Danahlia lies down beside Twinkaleni, curling around her protectively. Alice does her best to pass the time by tending their small fire and cooking up the rest of their birds. Kaliska awakens maybe two hours before dawn and ravenously munches on the small pile of leaves Alice had gathered for her. She stops when Alice asks how she thinks Twinkaleni is doing.

Kaliska's ears fall flat as she says solemnly, letting a few leaves drop from her mouth, "I've done all I can do."

"Does that mean she'll get better?" Alice asks.

Kaliska frowns, "Uh, some of her wounds were, pretty deep. I healed them, so she won't lose any more blood... but it's still pretty bad."

Alice's shoulder's sag, "What can we do?"

"We can ask Althea for help," the Chitali says hopefully, looking around, "I need to eat first, but we can try."

As Kaliska crams what's left of her greens into her mouth, Alice wonders what her Althea can do. Once Kaliska is finished, she motions for Alice to sit next to her beside Twinkaleni. She then takes Alice by the hand and places her other on the small mouse girl's chest.

Kaliska looks around again, her ears perked and listening, then she frowns, "I don't think Althea's around right now. We'll have to pray to her."

"Ok," says Alice uncertainly, but willing to try anything if it means helping her friend.

Kaliska smiles and holds Alice's hand a bit tighter. She then begins quietly, "Althea, we need your help. Our friend is hurt and I can't do anymore. She's hurt deep and I just, I can't reach in far enough. You have to, ok? I did what you wanted, so, you gotta help now too, ok?"

Kaliska gives Alice's hand an encouraging squeeze. Alice is surprised by the deer girl's words and doesn't really know how to add to them but she closes her eyes and tries anyway in the manner she was taught, "Please, Goddess Althea, hear our prayers and take pity on us. Grant us your blessing. Mend my friend's wounds so that we may continue our journey together."

Alice wants to go on pleading but Kaliska's grip on her hand has steadily been tightening and was now uncomfortable enough to make her look. Kaliska's eyes are wide and glow white, though her pupils look to have rolled back into her head. Her mouth is open in soundless surprise and the hand over Twinkaleni shakes violently, emitting a faint white glow directed to the Murin.

"Kali? Kali what's wro-" Alice is cut off by a strange tugging force across her entire body, as if she was lashed with a thousand thin strands of rope and being pulled toward the Chitali.

Kaliska's grip tightens painfully and Alice tries to free herself only for the pulling over her to change. It shifts, instead of pulling her entire body in one general direction, it now pulls her to where Kaliska maintains a crushing grip on her hand. Alice begins to feel as if some intangible part of her very being is getting sucked away by the Chitali. Afraid, she tries to scream for Danahlia, still asleep, only to have lost her voice. As Alice's energy drains rapidly from her body, she reaches desperately for the Liguna only to fall over, her strength gone and blackness consuming her.

Alice wakes the next day, the sun well into the sky. A weight on her leg alerts her to Kaliska laying partially over her. The Tokala gives the Chitali a shake but she's completely out.

"Hey," comes Danahlia's voice, the Liguna lay grinning in front of Twinkaleni, her lengthy tail reaching around to Alice.

Alice tries to rise but is immediately put back

down by a pounding in her head and a body full of aches and weariness.

She groans her discomfort and Danahlia asks, "Hey, you ok?"

"Ugh, what happened?" asks Alice.

"You fell asleep durin' your watch. We could 'a gotten eaten ya know?" Danahlia chides mildly, the end of her tail wiggling annoyingly about the fox girl's ears.

Alice strains to bat it away, "Ugh, how's Twinkaleni."

"Better I think. She woke up for second, just a little while ago."

The news invigorates Alice some, "Really?"

"Yeah, just for a sec, but I think she's on the mend at least."

Alice sighs in relief as Danahlia's tail comes poking about her ears some more, "Come on, get up. We gotta get movin' soon, it's already noon."

Alice grumbles at the idea and Danahlia crawls

over to Kaliska, "You too, Hooves. Up, up." After trying and failing to rouse the Chitali, Danahlia squats before Alice with some of their cooked bird meat, "Here, eat, you'll feel better."

Alice does without getting up and feels her strength begin to return to her. Meanwhile, Danahlia takes to poking and prodding Kaliska. The deer girl kicks her feet and swats at Danahlia's hands, slowly groaning awake.

"Stop," Kaliska whines at Danahlia, whose flicking at her ears.

The Liguna grins, "Geez, why are you guys so out of it today?"

This makes Alice pause, a memory blooming in her mind of Kaliska gripping her by the hand. The memory is faint but she remembers feeling afraid, and then terribly tired. Kaliska eventually gives up on sleep and Danahlia points out a generous pile of leaves she's gathered for the deer girl to eat. Kaliska's face sags and her ears droop but she does start munching on the greens. Danahlia wraps Twinkaleni up in the tarp, that she must have scrapped free of the dried cave algae, and ties the small Murin to her back. Once she has, Alice and Kaliska are reluctantly ready to travel as well.

They head roughly north, circumnavigating the cliff as they search for a new water source. Danahlia is in high spirits, though Alice and Kaliska only manage to shamble behind her. Alice asks but Kaliska seems to have no recollection of the previous night's events after they began to pray.

"She must have heard us and come to help," Kaliska offers cheerily, "Althea is so sneaky."

"Maybe," Alice says back. Danahlia's assurance that Twinkaleni is getting better makes it difficult to argue.

Walking late into the afternoon has yet yielded no water and with Alice and Kaliska trailing steadily further behind, Danahlia decides to finally call for a break. They drink little from their stores, trying to preserve what they have. Danahlia sets Twinkaleni on some grass and heads off to scout ahead. Kaliska lays her basket with the dragon egg to her side and plops down, quickly falling asleep. Alice sits next to Twinkaleni, determined to keep watch this time. She eventually settles beside the tiny Murin, laying her head down and stroking the soft gray fur of the mouse girl's brow. Watching her sleep makes Alice smile, then yawn, then rest her eyes, and finally nap.

A short time later, she wakes to Twinkaleni's large amber eyes watching her. The mouse girl blinks.

"Twinkaleni! You're awake!" cries Alice, reaching for the smaller girl.

The Murin tries to say something but only croaks. Alice gives her what's left of her water and Twinkaleni turns only enough to drink with aid. After she's had a few swallows, Alice gently glides her hand over Twinkaleni's fur, "How're you feelin'?"

Twinkaleni groans, "Exhausted. What happened?" Her eyes go wide then and she tries to rise, "Where's Danny?"

Alice catches her and lays her back down, "She's fine, just scoutin'. You had a little fall, but Kali's been healin' you so-"

"Those birds," Twinkaleni moans, her eyes looking like they're having trouble staying open.

"They're gone, everyone is ok," Alice assures her.

Kaliska's hand comes up to pet the Murin's

head, "She needs to rest."

Alice frowns but nods. "Just relax and sleep now. We're watching over you," she coos to the tiny mage.

Twinkaleni gives a weak nod as her eyes close and she quickly falls back to sleep.

Kaliska smiles tiredly, "She's getting better, but it's still going to be a little while before she's floating us around again."

"Is there anything we can do?" Alice asks.

Kaliska yawns, "Just wait."

Kaliska falls back to sleep as well but Alice, looking forward to telling Danahlia, stays awake and snacks on some of their store of bird meat. The Liguna returns before dark. Though she didn't find any water, she's cheered to hear of Twinkaleni's short bout of consciousness.

She's stroking the mouse girl's fur when Alice asks, "So what *did* you find out there?"

"Not much, just a lot of forest. We shouldn't have to worry about food though. Lots o' critters around. Kali say anything about Twinkie?" Danahlia asks.

Alice replies, "Just that she needs rest. I think the worst is over."

Danahlia sighs in relief and leans in to kiss the sleeping Murin on the forehead. The pair has their dinner, sitting close. The nights especially are getting cooler. After the meal, Danahlia suddenly puts an arm around Alice and pulls her in, rubbing her muzzle through the thick red-orange fur of Alice's cheek, the fox girl giggling.

Danahlia stops, asking into Alice's fur, "Is it just me or are you gettin' fuzzier?"

Alice smiles, "Yeah, I guess my winter coat's comin' in."

Danahlia's reply is a pleased noise and more cheek rubbing.

After the encounter with the birds, the girls aren't interested in taking chances, and decide it's best to post watch again. Alice let's Danahlia rest and takes the first shift, sitting close to her furless friend to shield her some against the cool night.

The party rises with the sun the next morning to continue onward, searching through the thick forest for water. They happen on a trail a few feet wide through the brush. It's suspected to have been made by some large ferals tromping along. The trail heads downhill, roughly in the direction they want to go, so they follow it. A few bare patches reveal large, round footprints along the path and the girls stop to examine them.

"Whatever made this was big and heavy," observes Danahlia, placing her own taloned foot over the feral made indention to compare.

"Yeah, but look," Alice points to the four stubby toes of whatever left the prints, "It doesn't look like it has claws. Maybe it's not a predator."

"We can always hope. These tracks aren't that old either, let's be ready for anything," advises Danahlia.

Alice nods and then looks to Kaliska a few feet behind them, "Kali, any ideas on what made these prints?"

The Chitali looks up, "Hmm?" She had just put the finishing touch on a smiley face she'd drawn in another of the large prints with the tip of one hoof.

"The prints, do you have any idea what made them?" Alice asks again.

Kaliska nods, "Oh yeah, something big."

"Big and maybe nasty. Here, you carry Twinkie," says Danahlia, untying the sleeping Murin from her back and retying her to the Chitali's chest, "If it gets dangerous, you get Twinkie outta there. Me and Alice 'll cover your back."

"But what if it's not? Wouldn't it be funny if it was a tiny feral with really big feet?" Kaliska asks, raising her arms to hold Twinkaleni so Danahlia can finish tying the tarp wrapped Murin to her.

"Yeah, hilarious," mumbles Danahlia.

Alice grins, drawing her sword, "We just wanna be prepared, just in case."

The girls follow the trail for a time. Steadily the tracks get more defined as they close on their maker. They can't see yet but begin to pick up short grunts from up ahead. Alice and Danahlia get low and ready their weapons, though Kaliska just keeps petting and cooing to the still slumbering Twinkaleni. Alice looks from Kaliska to Danahlia, who shakes her head and then stands as tall as she can to see over the lush grass around them. Alice follows suit, her fox ears angling toward the nearest grunts. Just over the grass in a clearing is a group of over a dozen large ferals.

The four legged beasts stand on the same large, flat feet the girls had been following tracks of. As Alice looks over them, she notes their thick, rounded, almost potato like, bodies and short brown to tan coats. Even on four legs, she imagines the biggest of them would probably come up to her chest. Their front and hind quarters look evenly proportioned unlike their slim tufted tails and large boney heads. Their long muzzles have knob like protrusions along them that look too rounded to be horns, with two beady black eyes overlooking them.

The large creatures are gathered around with their heads low and close to each other, kicking at something with their feet, while a few younger ones amuse each other by bumping and chasing one another.

Danahia whispers, "What do ya think?"

Still peering at the beasts, Alice whispers back, "Let's just watch for a minute."

Then Kaliska walks right past them saying, "Aww, look at the babies."

"Kali!" the others both whisper harshly, pulling back the deer girl by a shoulder each.

"Ugh, what?" Kaliska complains.

She's shushed but it's too late, the creatures all turn their large knobbed heads in their direction, small round ears angling with snorts of alarm. Danahlia clamps a hand over the Chitali's mouth as she and Alice hold her still. Parents position themselves protectively before their young and a few of the adults approach the girls, sniffing and grunting. Kaliska calms down as the nearest beast approaches cautiously, wide nostrils flaring as it takes in their unfamiliar scent. They stay frozen as it comes into arms reach, not wanting to seem threatening to the large creatures. Kaliska reaches for its nose and the beast jerks back a little when she touches it, but then it sniffs her hand curiously. Apparently feeling the girls offer no danger, the beast snorts dismissively and turns back to its herd. The ferals then resume kicking around at the earth.

Alice sighs in relief as she and Danahlia let Kaliska go. Kaliska looks at the hand snorted at, saying in disgust, "He snotted me."

"Yup, he got ya good," comments Danahlia cheerily, "But at least he didn't bite it off."

The girls come out of the tall grass and into the clearing slowly. They take the attention of some of the creatures, but most continue with whatever they're doing in the dirt. The younger ones, seeing potential new playmates, hurry over to the girls even as their mothers grunt angrily, quickly coming after them. Alice and Danahlia back away, but Kaliska kneels and extends her hands out to the excited youngsters, their tiny tails wagging. One mother approaches with warning snorts and threatens with lifts of her knobbed head. Kaliska ignores it, instead completely consumed with petting the four younger beasts that surround her, sniffing and grunting happily. The mother lumbers over, flanked by another, and sniffs Kaliska too. After a few flares of her nostrils, she seems to calm down and lets the deer girl play with her young.

Alice and Danahlia creep over then, very curious about the small creatures. The mothers eye them carefully, snorting, but making no move to interfere, extending the girls a remarkable level of trust. Alice crouches down, smiling at the bond Kaliska has somehow already made with these wild ferals. The little ones try to climb all over the Chitali, reaching their noses up to her face. Alice passes a hand over one, feeling its short soft coat and fleshy, somewhat loose skin. The small creature immediately turns to her, sniffing, its tail wagging furiously. She pets it some, which excites it enough to try to climb into her lap. Alice laughs looking up at Danahlia who leans over her shoulder grinning.

"Aren't they adorable?" Kaliska exclaims, watching the young beasts sniff at Twinkaleni.

"They are kinda cute, but they stink," says Danahlia, letting one sniff her hand. They do smell rather bad, like dead swamp grass, but their cuteness forces this aside for Alice.

A few adults begin making excited grunts that attract all the others, including the babies, causing the beasts to all bunch up around where they were kicking at the dirt. The girls watch uncertainly for a minute until a tiny trickle of water begins to run past the creatures' crowd of large flat feet.

"Huh, no way. The stinkers found water," says Danahlia.

The girls watch as the crowd of beasts grunt and snort happily at their discovery. It's difficult to see through the pressed bodies, but it seems like they managed to uncover a small spring. Excited but willing to be patient and let the creatures have the first drink, the girls settle in and try to come up with a name for the beasts. Names like stinkers, knob beasts, and potatophants are tossed around until Twinkaleni says they're ossicorns.

"Twinkie! Hey, how ya' feelin'?" asks Danahlia, the others surrounding the Murin.

Twinkaleni was laid on a patch of soft, thick grass, and is still wrapped in the tarp. She eyes the ossicorns, "Quite famished. Is there anything to eat?"

They offer her a piece of cooked bird and smile at her as she nibbles, holding the meat with her tiny pink hands. She looks around at them, "What?"

"We're just glad you're feelin' better," says Alice, grinning widely.

Danahlia leans in and kisses the Murin on the forehead, "Yeah, you were touch a go for like three days."

"Three, days?" Twinkaleni asks in surprise.

"Uh-huh, but we prayed to Althea and she

made you all better," adds Kaliska.

Twinkaleni considers, "I see. Well, give Althea my thanks won't you?"

Kaliska smiles and nods.

As the girls wait their turn, they share what's left of their water and have a light meal. Eventually, the ossicorns have their fill and wander away from the still bubbling spring to rest and eat the lush grass growing about. The younger ossicorns return with wet muzzles and muddy feet to play with Kaliska and investigate Twinkaleni, leaving Alice and Danahlia to gather water.
The adults have managed to dig out the spring enough to where it burbles freely into a small stream but is still very muddy. As they had done before, they use Kaliska's tightly woven basket and press it into the spring so the water seeping through the fibers is significantly cleaner. It's still brown, a bit gritty, and only the very bottom of the basket fills but it's the best they can do. Danahlia holds the basket down while Alice fills water skins. With water nearby, a decent bit of bird left, and Twinkaleni recovering, the party decides to rest for a while and help clean Twinkaleni's still stained and mattered fur.

Near evening, the family of ossicorns wanders away, this time heading east. Kaliska wants to follow them but the others say they need to continue north. They decide to stay for the night around the spring and get a fresh start in the morning. As they're discussing plans around a small fire, the dragon egg begins to hatch.

Chapter 4

Squiggles

Kaliska is curled up with the large, mostly scale covered egg beside the fire, pouting about the group's decision to continue north and not follow the occicorns. Alice and Danahlia are discussing hunting as they finish the last of their bird meat while Twinkaleni has fallen back into a slumber. While the Murin was still recovering, they would have to make do without her magic, which meant arrows were likely their best bet at another meal. But with their last having been broken in the battle with the vicious roosting birds, they would need to make more. The pair are toying with the feathers recovered from the two birds they felled and talking of finding some wood to make shafts when Kaliska startles them.

The Chitali bolts up, "Oh! Ohhh, it's happening! It's happening!!"

Danahlia mocks, "What? You're brain finally seeing the error of your vegetarian ways?"

"No. It's the thing, with the baby! It's happening!" Kaliska sits with her legs spread around the egg, pointing to it enthusiastically.

"What?" Alice asks in disbelief, immediately crawling over to investigate.

Danahlia follows and even Twinkaleni is roused by the commotion and comes to see. They eagerly watch for a few moments until the leathery end of the egg gets a sharp poke from the inside. The girls hold their breaths, eyes wide in wonder as it gets another, and another.

"Oh, he's coming, he's coming!" Kaliska practically squeals, clapping her hands in excitement.

The girls press their faces closer and closer together, watching intently as one last strong poke pierces the flexible shell and a tiny red nose pops out. It's nostrils are slitted similarly to Danahlia's, though it has a small stubby horn that reminds Alice of the prow of a boat. It quickly retracts and the girls look on in eager anticipation as it pokes through again, making the miniscule hole just a little larger. The striving infant does this several more times and with each thrust, more nose pops out, followed by a tapering muzzle, angular cheeks, and two golden eyes.

The fire light glitters off the wet looking scales

of the tiny reptile as it takes its first look around. Their faces are pressed so near each other that Alice can feel Danahlia's widening grin, her own mouth open in delight while watching the newborn dragon enter the world.

"Marvelous. Simply marvelous," exclaims Twinkaleni, tiny fists shaking at her chest.

"He's here, he's here," repeats Kaliska, sounding like she's only moments from bursting, her hands shifting uncertainly over the dragon's egg as if wanting to help but not knowing how.

As they watch, the baby dragon's head wobbles a bit as it looks to each of them. It blinks and the girls melt into oohs and awws. After looking around it starts to make a short throaty little noise.

Danahlia grins, "He's wonderin' which one of us is his momma." She then imitates the noise, taking the baby dragon's attention.

The others copy the dragon's call which seems to make it feel safe enough to try to pull the rest of its cramped body out of its protective shell. A slender neck of several inches steadily slides free before the infant catches on something. It tugs and wiggles a few times until Danahlia uses a claw to pull away a bit more of the flexible shell. This allows the baby dragon to get a shoulder free, then a tiny clawed forelimb. With it, the infant grips the ground, giving it the traction to pull out its other arm. Two claws to the earth, its body slides free next, revealing tiny wings matted like wet cloth tucked on its back.

The girls call encouragingly as the tiny reptile emerges further, but then catches again. Its long neck hooks back to look at the other half of its body, still trapped. It wiggles until a hind leg pops out. It's similarly clawed as its front two while being a bit thicker. With another look at the giants around it and a few more throaty sounds, the slick looking infant pulls it's other leg out along with a slender, lengthy tail. It crawls over to Danahlia and sniffs at her offered hand. It then looks up at her and makes its little noises again. She smiles and makes them back.

As the newborn peers around at the others, Danahlia announces, "Welp, looks like we got us a baby dragon."

Alice reaches for it and the infant looks to her hand. It's made curious by her fur, the dragon being covered in dark scales, and reaches for her fingers with its tiny claws. Alice places her hand before it on the ground. After some investigating, the dragon begins to climb up her arm. Its claws are very sharp and Alice can feel them pricking her even through her thick fur coat, but she can only laugh at the dragon's reaction to her.

"He's so cute!" exclaims Kaliska, running her fingers over its back.

Twinkaleni calls, "Estraleete," conjuring a bright grain sized speck of orange light so they can see the baby better as evening gives way to night. The infant takes great interest in the light and immediately doubles its efforts to climb up Alice in order to reach it. Alice laughs as the hatchling clambers up to her shoulder while Twinkaleni gets a closer look, then saying in awe, "I believe this is a Gullveigaryan."

"No, he's a dragon," corrects Kaliska, pointing, "See his wings?"

Examining the dragon closely, Twinkaleni goes on to say, "Gullveigaryans are a species of dragon, also known as 'witchbloods.'

"Witchbloods?" asks Danahlia, watching the tiny creature reach for the light by extending its neck, jaws open.

"Only time will tell for sure, but from its color and shape, I believe it is," Twinkaleni replies, lifting her magical light higher, "If it turns out to be so, we have done very well indeed in procuring it."

"He," insists Kaliska.

"Beg your pardon?" asks Twinkaleni.

"He's a *he*, not an *it*. I know, I felt it, even while he was still in his egg," says Kaliska confidently as she runs a finger down the dragon's long tapering tail.

The others look to the Chitali and Alice asks, "What's a 'witchblood'?"

"Well, from my personal research, I recall reading that Gulllveigaryans have a naturally high resistance to magic and are among the fastest flyers of all known dragons. These traits made them ideal for hunting rogue mages and countering magic wielders in battle. This, along with their deep red pigment, earned them their name."

"Rogue mages? Like you?" wonders Danahlia.

"I suppose so. Though this will make it, him, an

ideal weapon to use against the Order of Thermathrogi," the small Murin concludes.

The baby dragon has managed to climb up the back of Alice's neck and now has it's forelimbs atop her head as it snaps at the tiny ball of light, just out of its reach. After a few failed snaps, it belches a tiny wisp of flame at the magical light ball, snuffing it out.

Figuring the infant dragon is hungry, the girls wander about looking for something to feed it. Being reptiles, baby dragons do not drink milk and are equip to hunt and eat small things right away, Twinkaleni informs them. He seems to like the purchase he's found atop Alice and holds on tight when she tries to remove him. So, with the dragon nuzzling and sniffing about her ears, she scrapes a few bits of meat from their bird's discarded bones and dangles them before the infant on her head. The dragon swallows these eagerly.

Kaliska offers a few freshly plucked blades of grass but the dragon has no interest in them, prompting Twinkaleni to point out that dragons do not eat plants.

"He might if he knows how good they are," Kaliska counters and then waves her grass tantalizingly before the hatchling, eating some with exaggerated sounds of relish. The dragon remains unconvinced.

Danahlia manages to find some sort of beetle at the edge of their small fire's light and puts it on the ground. The moment the dragon spots the insect, it immediately climbs down from Alice to gobble it up.

"Eww! He ate it!" cries Kaliska.

"Course. That's protein. Gonna need lots to get big and strong, huh, little guy?" coos Danahlia.

The dragon eats similarly to a bird, swallowing the beetle whole. They can see his throat working on bringing the bug down and once it's gone he immediately starts to look for more. Alice and Danahlia run around in search of more insects to feed it, finding small ants, another beetle, and a cricket, while Kaliska tries to get the newborn to try some greens. As the girls feed the new addition to their party, they try to come up with a name for him.

"He's a Squiggles, just look at 'im," says Kaliska, as the dragon leaves her to chase after Danahlia and Alice.

To her credit, the dragon's body does squiggle as it walks, similar to how a snake moves from side to side over the ground.

Danahlia makes a rude noise with her tongue and Alice retorts, "We can't call a dragon 'Squiggles'."

Kaliska frowns, "Why not?"

"Because it's cruel," says Danahlia tossing another bug to the baby, who immediately homes in and swallows it, "What's gonna happen when he's older and goes up to a lady dragon saying, 'Hey, my name's Squiggles. What's yours?'"

Alice laughs, "Yeah, that won't end well."

Kaliska crawls after the dragon, "Well, if she's gonna judge him just by his name then she isn't good enough for our Squiggles."

Alice and Danahlia share a look, unable to counter, then Danahlia says, "I think a dragon needs a fierce name, like Ripclaw, or Razortooth."

Alice nods her agreement, "Yeah, like Crimsonwing, or just Red."

Danahlia points a finger to Alice, "I kinda like Red. It's simple and innocent on the outside but has that hidden sorta symbolism, like blood and ferocity."

Alice grins and looks over to Twinkaleni, who has been unusually silent throughout the exchange. The small Murin must have tuckered herself out even with the light use of her magic because she's curled by the fire, already asleep.

The baby dragon seems tired too, wandering over to the fire when Alice and Danahlia can't find anymore bugs in the growing dark. He yawns and seems to sluggishly look around for a place to rest. The girls gather around the fire to settle in as well though Kaliska seems to still have plenty of energy. As such, she's given first watch. Alice lies down and Danahlia quickly joins her, pressing herself against the Tokala's back and curling around her as they tend to like. Once they're comfortable, the dragon wanders over and curls up in the crook of Alice's arm. Kaliska whispers a prayer into her hands and then sends it up into the sky as if releasing a trapped butterfly from her palms.

Alice gently runs a hand over the tiny dragon, its head resting on its own tail like a pillow. His skin is very smooth and supple despite being scaled, almost like Danahlia's, and she can feel the ridges of bone just beneath. They're softer than she would have expected.

"He likes you 'cause you're warm," says Danahlia from between Alice's ears.

Alice looks up at her, "That the reason *you* like me?"

Danahlia snuggles her chin into the fur atop Alice's head, "Mmm, one of 'em."

The Liguna holds the fox girl a little tighter and they happily fall asleep.

In the morning, Kaliska is noticeably exhausted and it's revealed that she didn't wake anyone to relieve her of watch. She seems pleased however as she has somehow managed to get the baby dragon to answer to the call of "Squiggles." She refuses to say how but as the party moves on, the young dragon follows her around and seems especially excited when called to by the Chitali. Alice and Danahlia try to undo the damage, calling "Red," whenever they find something to feed him. With Kaliska tired, Twinkaleni still recovering but walking on her own, and their new baby dragon, the girls' pace through the mountain forest starts off especially slow.

Alice and Danahlia frequently scout ahead in search of food, leaving their companions to rest. On one such venture, the pair comes across a gathering of berry bushes crowded with birds and other small ferals. Even if they had arrows, the tiny beasts would be difficult to hit but they do their best to sneak up from two sides and try to catch something between them. When given the agreed upon signal, the girls burst free from the surrounding trees and charge, shouting and swinging their weapons in the hopes of causing a confused panic that will enable them to snatch some breakfast. The bushes explode with the frightened animals. So many that Alice can feel their fur on her legs and wings near her face. She even tries to snap at one bird with her own teeth, unable to get her sword up in time. Despite their efforts, both young hunters end up with nothing but the few berry bushes, nearly picked clean. As the pair picks what's left of the berries, the rest of the party joins them and the group decides to take a break, sharing the find.

Kaliska has taken to weaving fine string made from grass with her nimble fingers but quickly falls asleep against a tree mid weave. Alice roams around, chopping saplings with her sword for arrow shafts and Danahlia collects some pine sap to make glue for fletching, while Twinkaleni takes two rocks she's found to break a few emberstones into smaller bite sized chunks for the dragon. The infant eagerly gobbles up each of the faintly glowing stones she tosses him but quickly tires and curls beside the small mouse girl to sleep.

Alice, sharpening the end of a sapling, sees this and Twinkaleni smiles tiredly, "Digesting minerals no doubt takes a fair bit of energy."

Alice grins, continuing her work as the Murin joins the dragon in a nap. The berries they had are doing little to quell Alice and Danahlia's rumbling stomachs, so after a few arrows are ready, they decide to go on a hunt. It's not long before they come across some sort of apple tree being tended to by a large, but likely young, sand colored bear.

"Wow, he's big," whispers Danahlia, "If we can take 'im, we'll be set for a week."

"No, even if we could bring 'im down, havin' so much meat would just slow us down. Remember, we need to get north quick now that the dragon's here," Alice reminds, watching the feral stand on its hind legs to grasp an apple in its teeth.

"But... meat..." Danahlia whines softly.

"Not this time," Alice chides, and then has an idea, "But maybe we can get some apples."

After discussing Alice's plan, the girls split up and circle around to either side of the bear and its apple tree, sticking to the thick brush. Once in position, Alice makes as fierce and loud a roar as she can. Before the war had taken him, Alice's father had told her how some bears could be frightened off by loud noises. After a few more roars, Alice hears Danahlia make similar noises and takes a peak from behind the tree she had placed against her back. The bear is turned away from her, searching the trees cautiously. The pair continues their ruse until the bear decides it might be better to find somewhere else to snack and lumbers off into the forest. The girls cheer their victory and converge on the apple tree, filling their packs with the small, crispy, red fruits.

As the pair head back to find their companions, they hear them calling out their names but also calling for Squiggles. Fearing for their dragon, Alice and Danahlia pick up their pace, quickly finding a worriedly searching Twinkaleni and Kaliska.

"What's goin' on?" hails Danahlia as they approach.

"Where have you been?!" shouts Twinkaleni, putting her tiny fists into her hips.

"We went huntin'. Where's Red?" asks Alice, watching Kaliska still scanning the brush and calling for the dragon.

"He's wandered off," Twinkaleni informs them angrily, "You should have told us you were heading out!"

"You guys were sleepin'," argues Danahlia.

"Regardless," huffs the tiny mage, "we must make every effort to recover him immediately."

Agreeing to this, the girls fan out in the direction Twinkaleni said she last saw his footprints. A layer of fallen leaves and sporadic patches of grass make it impossible to know if he kept going this way but they remain hopeful and are soon alerted to the baby dragon's cries of panic. Racing to the sound, they see the infant fleeing toward them, crying out while futilely flapping his small wings. Bursting free from a bush just behind him charges a very large, black monster.

The creature chasing the dragon has two broad pincers held open before it on reaching arms. These are attached to a broad, armored body propelled by six swiftly scuttling legs that have the creature only inches from the frightened dragon's tail. The rear of the monster has a thick, segmented tail with a viciously curved stinger dripping with what Alice guesses is some sort of viscous, white venom.

"It's an eboncore scorpion!" warns Twinkaleni, "Mind the stinger, it has a deadly poison!"

Alice and Danahlia charge with weapons drawn while Kaliska bounds in ahead of them to snatch up the baby dragon, immediately fleeing with her precious cargo. The moment it realizes it can't get the dragon anymore, the scorpion raises its claws in defense only to have Danahlia impale it through the head so hard, her spear pierces through it, pinning the arachnid to the ground. Even so, its pincers grasp at her and its tail whips forth, stinging the shaft of her spear. Alice circles around, taking off its tail with a two handed swing of her broadsword, before moving on to remove its claws as well. With its weapons removed, the great scorpion slowly accepts its defeat and eventually stills.

Once they're fairly sure it's dead, the girls

converge on Kaliska to check on the dragon, who seems to want very much to contribute small puffs of flame to the battle. The Chitali swiftly looks over the squirming infant and relieves the others by saying he doesn't' look hurt. She then sets the dragon down. Immediately, he crawls over to the dead monster, extends his tiny leathery wings imposingly, and belches a little fire at it, causing one of its many round, black eyes to sizzle. Satisfied with this, the dragon crawls back to Kaliska and let's himself be picked back up.

As they ring the dead scorpion, Twinkaleni insists, "One of us must watch the dragon at *all* times. It would be a terrible loss to our cause were he to perish."

The others agree and have a few apples as they examine the monstrous creature. Its body alone is perhaps three feet long, with its legs, tail, and pincers making it look considerably larger. It has a few stiff hairs sporadically poking out from its shiny black carapace, which is remarkably smooth, almost to the point of being slick under Alice's free hand. The inner edges of the formidable pincers are jagged like serrated knives. But what really stands out is the bluish blood leaking from the creature.

Danahlia pokes at it with a toe talon, "Think

we can eat it?"

"Ew, you can't eat a monster!" declares Kaliska.

"Why not? We got it, we can do what we want with it," the Liguna counters.

"Didn't you say it has poison?" Alice asks Twinkaleni.

The Murin replies, "Indeed. The venom glands are in the tail but the book says this can be nullified with heat and be made safe to consume."

"Wags. Let's cut this guy up and get 'em over a fire," cheers Danahlia.

"We still have plenty of daylight left," Twinkaleni interjects, "I believe it prudent if we continue on before making camp."

"Yeah, we can carry some of it and cook it later this evening," Alice says to Danahlia's frown, "It'll give us somethin' to look forward to."

Danahlia concedes and Alice begins chopping the scorpion up. Kaliska assures them that she will not be dragging around any part of the monster, so

Alice and Danahlia laden her with their apples and pick the choicest cuts of arachnid, which they deem are the appendages rather than the body. Twinkaleni also takes a few leg segments for her backpack and the party moves on.

Making their way down the north eastern slope of the mountain, Alice wonders if Twinkaleni could make some sort of magical tracker for the dragon, similar to the one the agent of the Order of Thermathrogi used to track the mage herself. Twinkaleni feels this is a good idea and even says making such an item wouldn't even be that difficult. She uses the plant fiber string Kaliska had been weaving and ties a torn bit of cloth to one end. With the cloth, she collects a bit of the dragon's saliva, not a difficult task since he tends to drool a bit whenever one of the girls tosses him a tasty insect.

Once she has it, the tiny mage lets the string dangle from one hand, the cloth end hanging down, and focuses for a moment. Even as they walk, Alice can see the cloth end of the string drifting in the general direction of the dragon as if carried on an unfelt breeze.

Alice looks at the simple yet effective device in awe, "Wow, with that we won't ever lose Red again."

"Squiggles," Kaliska is quick to correct.

The Murin mage gives a brief smile, "It will do for now as long as the saliva sample is kept fresh," she then addresses the others, "Do keep an eye out for any shed scales or teeth. They will prove significantly more effective."

As evening draws near and talk turns to setting up camp for the night, Danahlia has already begun gathering fallen branches in eager anticipation of dinner. The party finds a small clearing and begins to settle in. Once enough fire wood is placed into a pile, Twinkaleni surprises everyone by blowing fire from her mouth.

She first crawls on all fours to the pile of sticks, then insures she has the dragon's attention by calling him Squiggles, the name he responds to the most. When she has it, she says, "Infermious," and blows into the center of the gathered pile. To the other's astonishment, a small puff of flame emerges just before her open mouth. It only lasts a second or two but is enough to set a few dry leaves alight and start the fire. Twinkaleni ignores the impressed comments of her companions in favor of repeating the word and blowing fire a few more times. The dragon flaps his tiny wings excitedly and makes little noises but doesn't participate. After a few more tries Twinkaleni gives it up and lets the girls throw on some pieces of scorpion.

"I didn't know Murin could blow fire," admits Kaliska.

"We can't typically, but I am a mage. I simply projected a fire spell from my mouth rather than my finger," Twinkaleni opens and closes her mouth as if trying to moisten it, "An unusual sensation."

"Wags. What's 'infermious'?" asks Alice, shifting a bit of scorpion leg over the fire.

"The command I'd like to use to order Squiggles to expel his fire," the small mage replies, "We should begin his training immediately. Dragons become considerably more difficult to train the older they get, thus starting early would be wise."

As dinner cooks, they discuss the training of their dragon. Teaching it to breathe fire on command is, of course, a priority, though other skills such as staying in one spot are also high on the list. Twinkaleni mentions that teaching the young dragon to fly may prove an interesting challenge as none of their party has wings.

"You think we'll really be able to ride him one day?" asks Alice, already envisioning herself soaring through the air on a great dragon's back.

Twinkaleni grins, "I don't see why not. It's been a while but dragons have carried people about in ages past."

"Flying would be nice. I always wondered what clouds tasted like," Kaliska chimes in, toying with the tiny dragon's tail as it intently watches Danahlia turning a scorpion leg over the fire.

As the scorpion cooks, its carapace changes from shiny black to a dull brown, while the meat turns from a milky blue to a creamy light orange. It has a sort of faint earthy smell to it, almost like boiling potatoes, and when Danahlia announces the first bits are done, Alice can't help salivating a little. A few browned legs are set aside to cool but the baby dragon has no patients and charges in.

Kaliska cries out, "No! It's too hot!" as Alice reaches for the swift reptile.

He evades her and dives head first into the steaming meat. Danahlia yanks away the cooked scorpion leg, burning her own hands with a pained cry. The dragon pops free with a wet squish just as he swallows a mouthful of meat and tries for more.

"It's alright," says Twinkaleni, "all dragons have an incredibly high resistance to heat. I doubt he even feels it."

The others look on and she seems to be right, the baby dragon eagerly swallows down more mouthfuls of scorpion without any sort of restraint despite the meat's obviously high temperature. Kaliska crawls over to heal Danahlia's singed hands while the girls watch amused as the dragon digs his head in deeper and deeper into the cooked scorpion leg, eating mouthful after mouthful with great enthusiasm.

Danahlia puts more scorpion over the fire and once the first batch has cooled enough, Alice, Danahlia, and Twinkaleni try it. The carapace has become brittle and must be cracked and peeled away to expose the soft sweet meat within. It reminds Alice very much of the giant crab they had back in the pixie forest in texture and flavor. It's very tender and tastes surprisingly good. The girls are able to eat their fill with a fair bit left over. Kaliska sticks to apples and leaves, giving a disgusted look when offered any scorpion. She also makes loud noises of pleasure while she consumers her vegetarian fair as if competing with the similar noises coming from Danahlia and Alice.

After their meal, the girls settle in for the night, the baby dragon curling up with Alice once more, his belly happily distended.

Chapter 5

Hunters

It takes over a week of travel for the party to finally be leaving the Great Horn Mountain behind. During this time, Twinkaleni recovers enough to confidently use her magic once more. The mouse girl makes great efforts to practice her water siphoning spell, which allows her to extract precious moisture from the abundant local flora for the party to drink. Despite the others telling her to take it easy, the tenacious Murin insists she must make up for lost time. This means she is often waving her arms around as she walks in a sort of gathering motion, while faint wispy mists reach out from passing trees and plants. The mage gathers these into tiny droplets about her hands before floating them before the trekking party. The other girl's and their dragon make a game of seeing who can gobble the most up.

Alice and Danahlia have conceded to calling the dragon Squiggles, or Squigs, after Kaliska had somehow managed to get him to respond well to little else. He has more than doubled in size since hatching and now walks beside the party for the most part, wandering off occasionally to investigate potential meals, but always returning in short order.

He and the girls have not gone wanting for food in the lively mountain forest, which Twinkaleni sites is a key reason for his rapid growth. They have even begun teaching the young dragon a few tricks.

Fire breath on command was naturally their priority and it didn't take long to figure out how to get the dragon to blow his tiny flames. While feeding him, it was found that if they held food just out of reach, Squiggles would get frustrated and try to knock down the morsel with his fire. After this discovery, it was only a matter of repeating the word *infermious* just before he blew his flame and then rewarding him with praise and food. His aim still needed work but he would now reliably blow a puff of fire whenever one had his attention, food, and called, "Infermious!"

While they travel, Alice notices Squiggles will often flap his wings while running or trying to look intimidating to the insects and small things he wants to eat, but he doesn't seem to flap them with any intent to fly. She wonders about this and Twinkaleni says that from her research before escaping the Order of Thermathrogi, she knows that dragons tend to learn to fly by watching and imitating other dragons.

As the heavy vegetation of the mountain forest

slowly gives way to flatter more open country, the party considers how they might teach little Squiggles to use his wings. They try to spot birds and alert the baby dragon to their presence so he might see how this flying thing is done. He seems interested but more in trying to catch them than learning from them. The girls also flap their arms enthusiastically while calling to Squiggles in an attempt to get him to imitate, though so far, this mostly just gets him to come to them and investigate why they're acting so strangely.

"How long do you think it takes a dragon to learn how to fly?" asks Alice, picking up the hefty reptile when he tries to climb up her leg.

Twinkaleni answers from beside the fox girl, "I'm not sure. I don't recall any of the volumes I've read on dragons mentioning exact times. It is likely subjective."

"Let's not have him learnin' *too* soon. He might just end up flyin' off," says Danahlia, walking in her usual lead position.

"He wouldn't just leave us," claims Kaliska, reaching over to pet Squiggles in Alice's arms, "He loves us."

"I suppose that is something we should take into account though," says Twinkaleni, rubbing one of her expansive ears between two pink fingers.

"What?" asks Alice, running her muzzle affectionately along Squiggles' neck.

Twinkaleni looks to the horizon, "The expanse we are to cross to reach the Gadara Mountains is sparsely populated but not uninhabited. If we could keep to the trees we should be safe but if Squiggles were to take flight in an open plain, even a small dragon might be spotted by someone."

"What if we just avoid any towns or villages?" Alice wonders.

"A wise precaution if we could manage it. But," the Murin says, looking down at her tattered shirt and torn pants, "we will need to resupply at some point."

Travelling through the mountain had been rough on the girls and what little they had with them. Clothes were ripped, backpacks straps were torn or barely hanging on, and they could all use a proper cleaning. Twinkaleni advises they continue on for a time, skipping the first and maybe even the second and third settlements they come across. The better to hide their trail just in case anyone was following.

"If the last anyone had heard of us is that we ventured into the haunted Great Horn, it might be best if rumors say we never emerged," concludes the little mage.

"That's good thinkin', Twinkie. 'Bout how far are those northern mountains anyway?" Danahlia asks over her shoulder.

Alice peers into the distance, "Well, we can't see 'em, so, far."

Danahlia grins and flicks her lengthy tail at her.

The party wanders on northward, ever in search of food and water. Twinkaleni's water siphoning magic was improving all the time, but even now it only yields a few precious drops. Not nearly enough to sustain four people and a growing dragon. Food is a slightly lesser concern as the mountain had provided it in abundance, allowing the girls a small store from which they eat as they search. Squiggles has little difficulty hunting the small lizards and occasional tiny, unwary ferals that inhabit the region and Kaliska does just fine dining on the tall grasses, but Alice, Danahlia, and

Twinkaleni are constantly on the lookout for something more substantial.

As their water supply begins to run dangerously low, Alice suggests something they had discussed earlier but were hesitant to put into practice. They thought of it while on the Great Horn but the thick forest canopy would have made it too dangerous. Now in the open, trees could better be avoided but the act still carried the risk of being seen. Still, their need is getting no less and one day, late in the afternoon, they decide it's as good a time as any.

Alice stands before Twinkaleni while the Murin focuses on her, the others looking about cautiously for any signs of people. They hadn't seen a soul since the riverside village of Fiske, but this was no reason to be careless.

As Twinkaleni works her earth magic with a mutter of, "Asendiote," she slowly raises a hand.

Alice steadily feels her own body weight diminishing. Soon she is so light she begins to float. Her feet leave the ground to slide along the overgrown blades of grass until she leaves those below as well. Alice remains calm, confident in the mage's power and skill. This was not the first time she had been sent skyward by it.

Squiggles becomes alarmed by the levitating Tokala and calls to her with short sharp cries while flapping his wings and standing on his hind legs, his fronts grasping for her. Kaliska rushes to quite the baby dragon as Alice floats on higher. The fox girl looks down, watching her friends shrink as she reaches the highest Twinkaleni had ever sent her and keeps on going. The gentle breeze rolling over the plains has her rocking and swaying unsettlingly but the mouse mage keeps her on course, both hands now raised to her.

The wind blows stronger for a moment and it nearly carries a weightless Alice off. She can feel Twinkaleni forcing her against the breeze, keeping her in place as she climbs steadily higher, now several stories in the air. Not entirely enjoying the experience at this point, Alice uses her new height to survey the land, looking for any signs of water, food, or civilization.

A ways off in the west, she spots a large herd of some sort of ferals. From this distance, Alice can only see them as moving specks of black and brown in the ember orange sunlight, but they look tall, much of their bodies being held above the long grass. Alice squints, trying to gather more detail in the waning light, but only sees that they vary in size. She pans her gaze elsewhere, seeing little more than a handful of massive trees breaking up the vast expanses of slowly yellowing grasses and a few lazily drifting clouds.

"See anything?" Danahlia calls up to her.

Alice hadn't realized it but she had shrunk into herself. Her feet are hooked around each other, legs together, tail tucked, and arms held close to her body. She points toward the ferals and calls down, "Yeah, a herd of somethin' over th-" A sudden gust blows hard and Alice sways frighteningly to one side, her arms flailing to keep balance.

"Alice!" cries Kaliska, Squiggles screeching in alarm at her side.

"Bring 'er down!" demands Danahlia.

"Be silent, all of you!" squeaks Twinkaleni angrily, both small pink hands held up with fingers splayed, trying desperately to maintain her focus.

Alice swiftly descends and lets out a breath of relief when her feet are once more on the ground. She plops down on her rump as her friends gather around asking if she's hurt while Squiggles tries to climb over her for his own assessment. Twinkaleni huffs breathlessly, doubled over in the grass, and Alice tells them she is fine and of the ferals she saw.

"We should check 'em out. They might be able to lead us to water like the stinkers back on the mountain," suggests Danahlia.

The others agree and head in the general direction Alice had seen them.

Coming across one of the particularly large trees sparsely scattered on the plain, the girls decide it best to make camp and pick up their search fresh the next day. They dine on their stores, not bothering with a fire, before scaling the thickly trunked tree and settling among its lower branches. Not knowing what predators may lurk in these lands, they decide it best to be safe than sorry. Squiggles proves to be an excellent climber, scrambling up with ease before crawling over Alice. He instinctively wraps his slender tail around a small branch before lying down just above her head, snuggling into her fur just as Danahlia usually likes to. Alice smiles up at him and quickly goes to sleep.

The next morning, Alice is awoken just before sunrise by Danahlia's tail poking at her back from another branch. The Tokala turns to her and yawns, smiling sleepily. Danahlia grins back and motions with a jerk of her head to climb down. Doing so alerts Squiggles, who follows the pair to the ground while Twinkaleni and Kaliska sleep on. Once among the dew damp grass, the pair sit beside one another and watch the sun peak over the horizon. Squiggles crawls around before settling over the girl's laps where he gets plenty of petting.

Danahlia leans over to Alice, "I had a dream about you last night."

"Yeah?" Alice asks, angling her fox ears toward the Liguna, "Was it a good one?"

"It was alright," Danahlia smirks.

Alice leans in, "What was it about?"

"Mostly this," Danahlia replies, wrapping an arm and tail around the fox girl's waist, pulling the Tokala in before rubbing her face into Alice's furry cheek.

Alice giggles, returning the affection until Squiggles notices and immediately tries to climb them, not wanting to be left out. They enjoy the sunrise and the warmth it brings before the others wake and it's time to start a new day.

After a small breakfast, the group sets back out in the direction of the herd Alice had spotted yesterday. There are more clouds today, though none look threatening, and with them is a near constant light breeze pushing from the north. It keeps the girls cool through morning and mid-day but makes it difficult for Twinkaleni to collect water from the grasses they march through. Instead she occasionally takes the wind and blows it in streams over Squiggles, who flaps his wings awkwardly as he fights the current. He doesn't seem to like it very much, snapping at the wind, but Twinkaleni feels the exercise will help strengthen his flight muscles.

By early afternoon, the party finally gets its first glimpse of the herd of ferals. It turns out that there are a number of different beasts making up the herd. The smaller among them look to be some sort of long legged deer. Gold coated, many have a pair of slender horns that curve back over their heads. The next tallest are creatures that vaguely resemble lumpy horses. They are of similar size to the equines but have great racks of antlers that extend far to the sides of their heads that look similar to a tree's branches. The largest in terms of sheer mass are beasts that look sort of like muscular cows. These creatures have massive shaggy heads and a pair of stubby gray horns with thick builds under dark brown coats. The girls gather behind an outcropping of pale gray, weather worn stone to plan. Twinkaleni suggests that their assembly here may mean water is nearby.

"Good, we can have our pick of the litter and get a refill," says Danahlia.

Alice nods though Kaliska protests, "No, don't kill them. They're not doing anything wrong."

Danahlia sighs as Alice replies, "We'll only take what we need, there are plenty out there. They won't miss one."

Kaliska frowns deeply, as she generally did when a hunt was being planned, but doesn't raise issue when she is reminded that Squiggles needs meat too. That settled, Alice and Danahlia leave Twinkaleni and Kaliska to watch over Squiggles, not wanting the young dragon to blow their approach. The pair stays low, the tall grass keeping them hidden while the breeze keeps their scent from the gathering of ferals. When they get close enough, they crouch in the grass and observe their prey from just over the blades.

"Second we make a move, they're probably all gonna panic and run," says Alice.

"Yeah," Danahlia agrees, "So let's make this count. How 'bout that one?"

Alice follows the lizard girl's pointing finger to a tan coated, white bellied buck. He's not the biggest of his kind and possesses modest horns, making her think he's probably still a juvenile. But he is the closest and grazes a little ways away from the herd, his tiny dark tail flicking periodically. Alice nods and nocks an arrow in her bow while Danahlia takes a two handed grip on her spear. As it had been for some time, Alice was to make her shot, hopefully slowing, if not killing the beast, so that Danahlia could rush in to finish it. This method had been successful for them many times and required no further communication on their part.

As Danahlia readies her charge, Alice sights her quarry and pulls back an arrow to her cheek. As she makes the swift calculations in her head to account for wind resistance, distance, trajectory, power, and where on the buck she intends to hit, a swift shadow races over the ferals. It spooks them, causing various cries of alarm to ring out from the beasts as they all begin to run away from the hunting pair. Confused and dismayed, Alice watches as their target flees, but then recalls the encounter with the large birds that had ravaged Twinkaleni so terribly and lifts her bow skyward, only to see some sort of large net falling over her.

The girls cry out as the net's weight falls on them and quickly tangles about their limbs as they struggle. Alice tries to reach for her sword, but the net restricts her movements so that all she can do is strain against its fibrous weave. Danahlia, enraged, shouts as she tries to rip the net apart, snapping a few strands while toppling the two over. As they squirm, an Ornivian lands nearby, glaring at them.

Alice had only ever seen a handful of the bird people back in Toki village, her former home. None of the rare winged folk had lived there but occasionally one or two would stop in to trade for supplies or rest. The few times Alice had seen them, they never appeared hostile despite often possessing large, taloned feet and sharp, powerful looking beaks. This one, however, did not seem happy to see them at all.

Her colors are drab shades of light brown interlaced with tan and white. Despite being covered with feathers, she has a smooth roundness to her figure, which becomes more so as she folds her exceptionally long, winged arms back, exposing the three fingered hands she has about midway down her wings, somewhat like where a bat has its thumbs. Her beak is mostly yellow, thick, perhaps half a foot long, and hooked near the end. She is white chested and wears loosely hanging leather garments that only just keep her modesty. She also wears a variety of colorful beads that hang mostly from around her head in short braids. Alice might think she was quite pretty if the Ornivian's large, round, milky blue eyes weren't glaring at her with such ire.

The bird girl takes three short hops toward the trapped pair caught in her net. She does so on very large taloned feet, featherless, yellow, and almost scaled in appearance. Her talons are black and viciously curved, vaguely similar to Danahlia's. Danhalia herself, growls to be set free upon seeing the girl but Alice only watches. The girl ignores the Liguna, looking over her catch with quick, very bird like jerks of her head.

She steps a bit closer to Alice and demands in a rapid, irritated, but youthful tone, "Who are you? Who are you? Who are you?" each question accompanied by another swift jerk as if to inspect her prisoner from different angles.

"Let us out o' here!" Danahlia roars, getting her toe talons involved with ripping the net apart more.

Alice elbows Danahlia hard in the ribs, thinking it best to buy time until there friends got to them. She assures the bird girl, "We're nobody, just travelers."

"Ruined the hunt you did, you did you did," accuses the bird girl angrily, bobbing her head.

Another, larger, Ornivian swoops down with speed and grace to land beside the other. This one is also female, looking and dressing very similarly to the first though with more matured features. She has a mild reddish tone to her overall coloring and a bit of dark gray at the end of her beak.

"Ruined the hunt *you* did, little one," the larger says sternly in a strong, feminine voice to the younger.

The smaller of the two recoils from the words as if they could injure her. "No, followed direction I did, I did I did," she insists back.

"Direction was to wait in shadow of the cloud. Hide your own shadow it would have. Too impatient were you, too impatient as always," admonishes the bird woman, her wings half tucking back to reveal two long knives with curved white blades in her hands.

She approaches Alice as the younger one turns away, revealing her long feathered tail.

Alice cries, "Wait, we didn't mean to-" but the more mature of the pair grabs the edge of the net in one taloned foot and begins to flap her massive wings, taking to the air.

Doing so kicks up dust, forcing Alice to close her eyes, but she feels the net being lifted from her and does her best to untangle herself from it. The gust lessens enough for Alice to open her eyes and she finds Danahlia and herself freed. They both get to their feet immediately as they watch the bird woman drop the net near the bird girl's feet before landing once more.

The girl looks over her net and then to Danahlia, practically screaming, "Ripped it you did! You did, you did!" before the more mature Ornivian extends a long arm before her.

"Serves you right, Feathers," Danahlia shouts back while hoisting up her spear, not threateningly but making it obvious it was there, "You're lucky I didn't just shred it all to pieces."

The smaller of the bird people lets out a piecing hawk-like screech and begins beating her wings in anger, but the larger keeps her grounded, saying, "Store your energy for the hunt. Mouths we have to feed."

"The net, the bare one-" the bird girl begins to protest but a sudden intense gaze from the larger silences her.

The bird woman then takes to the air with a few beats of her impressive wings as the younger grabs her torn net in her talons and turns to follow.

Before she takes off, she looks back at Danahlia and Alice to warn, "Be watching you I will, I will I will."

She then ascends into the air in the direction of the larger and the fleeing herd of ferals. As the pair look after the Ornivians, shrinking into the distance, and dust themselves off, Danahlia grumbles darkly about the bird people ruining *their* hunt and then having the nerve to blame *them*.

"Are you two alright?" Twinkaleni's voice sounds from somewhere.

Alice looks around and spots the Murin's

expansive ears peaking just over the tall grass, "Yeah, we're fine, I guess."

"No, we're not! Those feathered, lice carryin' tick bats cost us our dinner!" shouts Danahlia, pointing with her spear, clearly still agitated by the situation.

"At least they didn't freak about you bein' a cold blood," says Alice.

"Indeed," agrees Twinkaleni, "we *must* be more cautious. Hopefully they will not feel the need to tell others of us."

"Maybe we should just go take 'em out," seethes Danahlia, her tail flicking behind her, "A little magic, a few arrows-"

"Don't be foolish," the small Murin admonishes, "Perhaps we can use this encounter to our advantage."

"Use how?" asks Alice, looking after the bird people but seeing only open sky and a few clouds.

"The larger of them mentioned they had mouths to feed. Judging by the immaturity of the smaller, they may be short on hunters and thus food," explains the mouse girl after a few moments of rubbing one of her ears, "If we could secure a surplus, we may be able to work out a mutually beneficial arrangement."

"Yeah, and after you ruined that girl's net, they're gonna have an even harder time huntin'," says Alice to Danahlia.

The Liguna smirks proudly, tapping a clawed finger to the side of her head, "See, was already five steps ahead."

Alice rolls her eyes and looks to Twinkaleni, "They might know where water is, or at least could find it faster from the air."

Twinkaleni nods, "My thoughts exactly, but to get any cooperation we *must* bring down one of those beasts."

In agreement, the girls hurry back to Kaliska to see if she's managed to keep watch over Squiggles alone. It turns out this didn't even merit concern. When they find the Chitali, she has the baby dragon on his back, batting playfully at her hands while she rubs his paler scaled belly.

Her leaf shaped ears perk up as they near and

she looks them over, finding they've come back empty-handed, "Oh good, you didn't kill anything this time."

The hunters choose to ignore this as Squiggles races over to investigate. He seems disappointed that they hadn't brought him anything. They explain the situation and immediately head after the herd of ferals, feeling it is likely their best chance at a large kill. Alice asks if Twinkaleni knows anything about the Ornivians, her own knowledge of them limited to only a few sightings.

The Murin says she recalls very little of them from her studies when she was still training with the Order of Thermathrogi. From what she remembers, there are many different groups of Ornivians, though all tend to be rather nomadic and have few permanent settlements. For the most part, they tend to side with the Warm Bloods in times of major conflict, but this is mostly for their own protection rather than them having any actual stake in such things. Even so, they are still highly valued as scouts and message carriers, though their numbers are generally so few that they rarely take a distinctive role in battle.

After seeing how easily Kaliska had looked after Squiggles alone, Twinkaleni decides to join the hunting party once the girls have caught back up to the herd of ferals. They crouch behind a few large rocks and a hardy bush to observe the gathering of beasts, mostly munching on grass.

"Think we can get one of those big ones now?" Danahlia quietly wonders, peering from behind the rocks.

"Maybe, but they look strong. Let's get one of the smaller big ones," whispers Alice, preparing her bow.

"I believe those are some species of bison," informs Twinkaleni, "The guide book has an entry. They are known for their strength and foul tempers."

Alice adjusts an arrow's seating on her bow's string, "Strength means muscle, and muscle means-"

"Meat," Danahlia finishes hungrily, "If we can get one, we'll be set."

The girls periodically look skyward for the Ornivians, but only see a few scattered clouds floating in a sea of orange. The waning daylight tells them that this will be their last chance to get a kill today. Alice spots a young bull straying a little ways from the mass of ferals and points it out to her companions. They discuss their plan and now ready to put it into action.

Alice stands slowly, drawing her bow. Just as she fires, she shouts, "Now!"

Taking her cue, Twinkaleni raises a tiny pink hand to the rocks they hide behind and lowers her other hand to the bull with a call of, "Gravitus!"

Danahlia charges toward the beast at a full sprint, her spear raised, and shouting like mad to frighten the other ferals. As expected, the herd begins to stampede away from the potential danger with cries of alarm and the loud rumble of many hooves. The girl's target, now with an arrow in its front side and unable to flee with Twinkaleni's earth magic transferring the weight of the large rocks onto it, turns to its aggressors. With a startlingly deep bellow, it begins to charge at Danahlia the moment it spots her.

The pain from the arrow sticking just below the bison's shoulder seems to lend it strength as it manages a surprising speed despite Twinkaleni's spell. The stones before her begin to shake free from the ground and even float as Alice sees the mage focus more of their weight onto the enraged beast. Alice herself fires a few more arrows, scoring several hits, but each only seems to anger the charging mass of muscle and horns further. Danahlia has to dive out of the way to avoid being trampled. The monster charges past the Liguna and then spots Alice's movements, adjusting to line her up next.

"I... can't... hold it," Twinkaleni gasps through clenched teeth, her fingers crooked and still stretched toward the beast and the rocks.

Alice fires one last arrow at the beast's head as it closes the distance with frightening speed. The merely wooden point can't pierce its thick skull and shatters on impact. She hears Danahlia somewhere shout a warning, the charging beast only yards away.

Alice is torn between sticking by the Murin and leaping to safety when Twinkaleni switches tactics with a panicked cry of "Asendiote!"

The rocks slam back into the ground with a resounding thud that nearly knocks Alice off her feet. The bison lifts just off the ground, its legs still kicking, as it cries out, its momentum rocketing it toward them. Alice grabs the small mage to her chest and pulls her back with her as she kicks backward from the ground, diving behind the newly planted rocks. She lands hard and the Murin's weight knocks the wind from her but she still manages to see the enraged beast sail only inches over them, a thick, pointed hoof clipping her still bent knee.

Alice yips, pain blooming along her leg, but she tries desperately to ignore it, kicking at the dirt while trying to rise with Twinkaleni to hide behind the rocks before the beast can turn toward them again. The bison lands awkwardly but manages to get back to a stand. Before it can turn, a piercing hawk's cry echoes from above and the Ornivian woman lands her full weight atop the bison's back. With only a flash of movement the woman leaps off, taking to the air once more. The young bull isn't deterred and turns to Twinkaleni and Alice, the girls still scrambling to find their feet.

Alice's knee screams with pain and she tries to keep it straight, making due with one leg while still holding on to a squirming Twinkaleni. Alice watches wide eyed as the bison finds them again, its neck pouring blood onto its thick fur, its breathing ragged and accompanied by puffs of steam from its nostrils. Just as it starts toward them again, Danahlia flies into its side, driving her spear and both taloned feet into its flank. She kicks off as hard as she can, falling into the grass, but it's enough to topple the heavily wounded beast, causing it to tumble over in the opposite direction with a surprised grunt.

Alice can bear it no more and let's Twinkaleni go, sliding back to the ground with pained whimpers. Danahlia finishes off the bison with a few more stabs of her spear before rushing over to check on her companions.

"Geez, that guy didn't know when to give... oh ticks, what happened?" asks Danahlia, kneeling beside the hurt Tokala.

Alice can only grit her teeth in pain, holding her knee, so Twinkaleni replies, "I believe she was struck by the bison."

Twinkaleni and Alice jump when Danahlia screams, "KALI! Get your weed-eatin' butt over here!"

Chapter 6

Predators

A few moments later, Squiggles appears and starts to climb over Alice, his head poking around to see what the matter is. Twinkaleni pulls him away as Danahlia looks around for the Chitali.

She spots her looking at the pair of bird people, who now stand near the downed bison, and shouts, "Kali! Here! Now!"

Kaliska turns from the Ornivians and bounds over to the girls, "What?" When she spots Alice she immediately drops to the fox girl's side, "Oh, what happened?"

Through gritted teeth, Alice gasps, "My knee, I think it's..."

"Ohhh," Kaliska frets, "Lemme see."

Alice gingerly removes her hands from her knee to reveal torn trousers and blood staining the sunset orange fur beneath. Kaliska takes in a hissing breath.

"Do somethin'," Danahlia urges impatiently.

The deer girl then moves a probing finger toward the wound asking, "Does this hurt?" just before touching it. Alice screams and swipes at the Chitali's forearm with her nails, only missing because the deer girl jerks away. "Ok, ok. Now we know," says Kaliska, her palms out in surrender.

Alice falls back into the grass, letting her anguished gasps turn to whimpers as Twinkaleni asks, "Can your magic heal her?"

"I don't know. But I can try," Kaliska says, clapping her hands twice before rubbing her palms vigorously together.

Her tongue slowly pokes out of the side of her mouth as she warms up. She then extends her hands toward Alice's injured leg. The searing, stabbing pain racing out from her knee slowly lessens to an uncomfortable throbbing heat. The Chitali then moves her fingers closer.

"Don't!" Alice hisses through her teeth.

Kaliska moves closer, "I gotta see if it's broke."

"Can you heal broken limbs?" asks Twinkaleni, struggling to keep hold of a squiggling Squiggles.

"Um, yeah. Maybe. I think so," Kaliska nods, her words steadily less confident.

"Ugh, maybe it'll get better on its own, let's just give it a day and see," suggests Alice, her apprehension building rapidly.

"At least let me try," Kaliska whines, "I can probably do it. Just, don't move."

Kaliska sends a probing finger toward Alice's wound once more. Expecting another horrific jolt of pain, Alice is about to cry, "Don't!" but the word gets caught in her throat when she feels the deer girl's finger on her knee. It doesn't hurt. Alice can sense Kaliska feeling over her and even pushing a bit, but there is no pain, only a sort of disembodied sensation almost as if it isn't even her knee being examined. Alice looks on, equal parts surprised and curious.

The larger Ornivian makes her way toward the girls with cautious steps. This alerts Danahlia who looks up to the bird woman, then past her to the younger one, who is now closely examining the downed bison, too closely for the Liguna's taste.

"Hey, that's ours!" she calls, rising with her

spear to confront the younger Ornivian.

"Saved you we did, we did we did," the bird girl throws back and the two begin to argue over who has rights over the kill. The larger Ornivian ignores them to watch the Chitali work.

Kaliska adds more fingers, poking, pushing, and rubbing spots. Alice observers with gritted teeth, expecting at any moment for the pain to return though Kaliska's magic seems to be keeping it at bay. The deer girl starts to talk to herself while she works saying, "Sss oh, that should probably be more like this. And these, are ok. That one's just a little pulled."

As Alice looks on, Squiggles frees himself from Twinkaleni's grasp and plants his foreclaws on the Tokala's stomach. He then spreads his little wings and hisses angrily at the bird woman who's moved to loom over Kaliska to observe. Twinkaleni tries to take hold of the protective infant once more but it's too late.

The Ornivian woman's yellow eyes widen, "A dragon?"

Alice immediately says "No," as Twinkaleni gets hold of Squiggles. He flaps his wings in her arms, trying to get free as he snaps wildly at the stranger.

"Don't, don't be ridiculous," Twinkaleni blurts, trying to keep hold of the struggling reptile, "Everyone knows, ugh, dragons have been extinct for centuries. A mere birth defect- (Twinkaleni cries out as Squiggles scratches her in his squirming) gave this poor salamander the appearance of having wings. Vestigial I assure you, entirely vestigial. We found it and took it as a pet."

"Uh, yeah, we found him. He can't fly," says Alice in an effort to confirm Twinkaleni's story.

The bird woman moves to examine Squiggles closer only to have him puff a burst of flame at her. She jumps back in surprise as Twinkaleni drops Squiggles, who immediate returns to his post on Alice's tummy.

"Uh, yes, as a salamander, he can also blow fire. A common trait among there kind," the Murin assures, looking at the scratch on her arm, "Salamanders I mean, not dragons. He isn't a dragon. Clearly."

"Saved it," says Kaliska, smiling over to Twinkaleni before returning to her work on Alice.

The bird woman looks questioningly at the girls and Squiggles.

"Yes. Yes? You saved Alice's leg? Wonderful news, well done," congratulates Twinkaleni lathering on enthusiasm, desperate to change the subject.

Kaliska starts, "Oh, I wa-"

Twinkaleni immediately interrupts with, "Yes, *very* well done! Alice, how does it feel?"

Alice looks into Twinkaleni's strained gaze and says, "Uh, ok I guess. Did you heal it, Kali?"

Kaliska gives Alice's knee a look at different angles, sniffing while still feeling over it, "I think I got most of the squishy bits, but the bone has a tiiiny crack. It's gonna be tender for a little while."

Relieved, Alice nods and watches as the Chitali continues to finger about her knee, the numbing sensation of her magic slowly wearing off to leave a throbbing ache in its wake.

The bird woman raises her beak to them, "Mmm, not a dragon. Shame. My people have revered dragons long before your wars with the bare ones drove them away. To find a dragon still living in this age would be worthy of grand celebration," she looks to Squiggles standing guard over Alice and smirks, "And anyone who could earn a dragon's loyalty would be greatly admired."

Twinkaleni and Alice share a look before the Murin says, "Uh, a shame indeed then that this is not a dragon. Alas, it is widely believed that they are gone for good from these lands."

"Mmm," is all the bird woman replies before swiftly turning away and calling to her smaller companion, "Weiya! We go."

The smaller hawk girl, Weiya, turns from Danahlia, the pair nearly coming to blows, and cries, "But the meat. Owe us they do! They do they do!"

"Enough. We will get our own," commands the Ornivian woman as she unfolds her wings.

"Wait!" Twinkaleni squeaks, giving the woman pause, "We, had hoped that we could ask for your aid. We would, of course, be willing to exchange a portion of the bison for it."

This seems to interest the Ornivian, who turns her head back to the Murin with a swift jerk, "What aid do you need?"

"We need water," admits Kaliska glumly, having just drunk the last of hers from a waterskin.

"Yes, if you know of a river or lake, even a pond, we would gladly share our meat with you for your knowledge of it," says Twinkaleni.

The hawk woman looks to Danahlia and Weiya glaring at each other over the bison as she considers. "Mmm, no rivers or lakes. Closest is stream, northwest. Not far to fly, but a walk of days," she says pointing with a wing in the general direction the herd had fled.

"Thank you," says Twinkaleni gratefully, she then looks to Danahlia, "Let them take what they want."

Danahlia looks questioningly at her friends, then receiving a nod from Alice, steps away from the kill and returns to them, the butt of her spear knocking hard into the earth with each step, tail held high.

Alice tests her knee. It still hurt a fair bit but nowhere near as much as before.

Danahlia asks, "How's your leg?"

Alice smiles up at her while giving Squiggles a pet, "Feels a lot better now. Thanks Kali."

Kaliska grins and shakes her fists and hips in a little dance, singing, "Yup, yup, yup yup yup, yup yup, yup yup yup."

Danahlia raises a brow at the Chitali and then looks distastefully back to the Ornivians, crouching over the bison to discuss what they want to take from it. "They saw us *and* Squigs now. If we wanna keep our scent off the road, this might be our only chance," the lizard girl says coldly.

Alice's eyes widen, "What? What're you talkin' about?"

Kaliska sniffs herself and then her robe, "I don't smell *that* bad."

"I'm sayin' if we wanna keep *anyone*," the Liguna says with a nod back at the bird people, "from tellin' anyone *else* about us, this might be the best time."

"Are you?" Alice starts and then quiets considerably, "Are you talkin' about... killin' 'em?"

Kaliska looks shocked as Danahlia turns back to her companions, "I'm just sayin', if we need to, this might be our best shot. Thought the point o' headin' north was to go invisible for a while."

"We should discuss this more before making any rash decisions," advises Twinkaleni.

Alice shakes her head, "No, we can't go around killing people just because they might talk to someone about us. That's crazy."

"No! You can't!" shouts Kaliska.

She wants to stand and get more out but Danahlia swiftly subdues her by pressing her body down on the Chitali's back and holding a hand over her mouth. Kaliska struggles some, but the other's collective shushing gets her to stop. The Ornivians look curiously over from their carving of the bison.

The girls that can, smile innocently back at them, Alice even giving a little wave as Twinkaleni calls to them, "Take as much as you wish. We are simply so grateful for your help."

The bird people look to each other before resuming their task, muttering something about spending too much time in the dirt.

"Ticks, Kali, we're not doin' anything yet. We're just talkin', ok?" Danahlia whispers hoarsely into her captive's ear.

The deer girl shakes her head and makes disagreeable noises through the Liguna's hand.

"Let us discuss our options carefully," encourages Twinkaleni.

"No, no, we're not becomin' murderers," insists Alice.

Kaliska muffles something that sounds like agreement.

"It's not like these would be our first," says Danahlia, reminding the others of the deserter from the pixie's forest, the vile agent sent after Twinkaleni from the Order, and even the would-be robbers at the Bear's Den. This is the first Kaliska has heard of this and seems alarmed by the Liguna's words.

"Those were in self-defense!" Alice shoots back as loudly as she dares.

"It could be argued that this too is in self-defense," says Twinkaleni, "*Preemptive* self-defense

I suppose would be more accurate."

"Look, here's how I see this playin' out if we do nothin'. We let 'em go, they tell their friends and who knows who else we got a dragon. They come back in numbers, kill us, and take 'im," Danahlia explains, looking to Squiggles.

Twinkaleni rubs one of her ears thoughtfully, "Even if we do eliminate these two, others of their kind are sure to come looking. It will not be difficult for them to spot us from the sky while we are in the open like this. And we do not know of any shelter nearby."

Danahlia eventually let's Kaliska go after assurances that she will keep her voice down and the girls argue over the matter for a time. Alice and Kaliska are against even considering it, Danahlia argues that it is for their own safety, while Twinkaleni remains torn on the issue. The girls are so engrossed in their discussion that they don't even realize the Ornivians have gone until Twinkaleni points this out. Settling the heated debate, they move on to investigate the bison.

The feathered pair left much of it behind, though they took its hide. Danahlia quickly gets to work on taking the remaining meat. As she generally did when any butchering was afoot, Kaliska wanders off to find her own supper. This leaves Alice and Twinkaleni to get a fire going.

Unfortunately for them, the plains are void of trees save for the occasional giant one, but none were in walking distance now. Alice decides to dig a fire pit so they can use the abundant grasses around them and Twinkaleni gets the idea to try her water siphoning spell to further dry out a few patches. While she pulls the moisture from yellowing blades of grass with gestures that look as if she's trying to collect the air itself, the grass fades further, becoming brittle and easy to collect. Twinkaleni dumps the dry grass into the hole Alice dug and once Danahlia has a chunk of meat ready, they get Squiggles to light the fire.

As they had expected, the grass burns much too quickly and has the girls running around trying to keep it going. Already tired from the day's events, they don't bother cooking more than they immediately need, though they find their efforts are well worth it. The bison meat turns out to be surprisingly tender, lean, and sweet. Kaliska frowns at her companions' frequent sounds of relish as they and Squiggles eat. By the time dinner is over, it's well into dark and the party curls atop the thick grass to sleep, Danahlia taking first watch.

Alice is awoken in the middle of the night to Twinkaleni shouting, "Estraleete!" A blinding, fist sized, moon white, light blossoms over the Murin mage.

Mind still foggy from sleep, Alice mumbles, "What is it?" as the others awaken as well.

"We are not alone," says Twinkaleni, looking into the darkness beyond her light and pulling free her miniature needle like rapier.

From the night comes a noise, a strange noise, one Alice had never heard but still felt she could place. It was the laughter of insanity, dark, ugly, and completely devoid of humility or grace, the kind of laughter that might leak from a mad man just before he did something truly awful. Alice's ears angle and she turns to the sound, peering into the blackness beyond Twinkaleni's light. She finds two shining green eyes looking right back at her. The laughter gains a collaborator and another pair of eyes joins the first, then another and another. Alice pans her gaze around as more maniacal laughter echoes from the darkness, revealing that the eyes are everywhere.

Danahlia takes up her spear and turns to face the closest, asking with nervous anger, "What are they?"

"Nasties," Kaliska replies, scooting toward Twinkaleni.

Alice moves to unsheathe her broadsword only to have a sharp pain in her knee give her pause but only for a moment. She stands shakily with Danahlia and Twinkaleni, Jellybane gripped tight in both hands.

Twinkaleni shouts, "Estra Mishraities!" causing her light orb to burst silently into thousands of glittering particles that she sends all about them and into the crowd of eyes. Not as bright as their predecessor, the glowing dust's dimmer illumination covers more ground and reveals the threat all around them.

More than a dozen shadowed shapes lurk in a loose ring around the frightened girls. They're not overly large, standing perhaps a foot off the ground, but they clearly have numbers on their side. In the dim light, they appear to be quadrupeds with large heads, powerful jaws, and mangy dark coats. Squiggles hisses at them, flapping his wings threateningly, but Kaliska grabs him up before he can do anymore.

Alice tells her friends, "They probably just want the bison. We should go."

"No, it's ours," counters Danahlia, holding her spear point toward the nearest of the beasts.

"Don't be foolish," rebukes Twinkaleni, "Kali can't fight, Alice can barely stand, and I can do little while holding this light. You can't possibly take them yourself."

"I can try," Danahlia grumbles, readying a thrust.

"Danny! We can get another bison. Let's let this one go," pleads Alice, not wanting to see the Liguna lose any more than her pride.

Danahlia looks as if she might attack anyway but eventually grunts, "Fine. Can you walk?"

Alice thinks she can but after a few steps, she realizes that her injured leg simply won't be taking her very far. She limps on after Kaliska as Danahlia and Twinkaleni cover their slow retreat. The creatures do not pursue, their mocking mad laughter growing louder as they converge on the bison to feed.

Once the girls feel they are out of immediate danger, they wander on for a time in the dark. Danahlia carries Alice on her back but not alone. Twinkaleni holds a small orb of concentrated star and moon light ahead of the party while simultaneous lowering Alice's weight with her earth magic. Still recovering from her earlier magical exertions, the Murin mage takes only a portion of Alice's weight, distributing it around them. The extra gravity pulls down the grass in a circle, making it look as if they travel in the footprint of some invisible giant. After an exhausting hour or so of this, the girls once more settle down to sleep.

Alice is on last watch. She lies back, propped on her arms, trying not to bend her leg as the sun begins to rise, spreading its glorious rays over the plain. Squiggles has joined her and nuzzles around hopefully for food while Alice lets the others sleep in. Thanks to the night creatures, the small party is not only alarmingly low on water but food as well.

Once the others start to wake up, Kaliska takes another look at Alice's leg and does her best to heal it a bit more, though she admits the bone is simply going to take time to mend completely. They have what's left of their stores for breakfast before getting underway. As they move on in the direction the Ornivians said water was to be found, Danahlia occasionally runs off to scare the still present members of the feral herd along with them in the hopes of having food and water at their eventual destination.

The group is resting in the afternoon when they spot familiar shapes soaring toward them in the sky. They ready their weapons as the bird people from yesterday approach. The winged pair land without hostility and have even come bearing several gourds in their taloned feet. They offer them to the party and the girls find that they are filled with precious water.

After a sniff, Alice, Kaliska, and Twinkaleni drink greedily though Danahlia asks suspiciously, "What's all this for?"

The larger of the two says, "Long walk to the stream."

Weiya grins widely, "Saved you again, we did, we d-" but a stern look from the bird woman silences her.

The larger then continues, "We need more meat. Hunting will be easier with more hunters."

After a large gulp of water, Alice asks, "So, you

help us and we help you?"

The Ornivian woman nods, and Weiya says excitedly, "More for all this way, see see see?"

The girls decide the arrangement will work for now and proper introductions are made. The larger Ornivian is called Lolani and says she is Weiya's aunt. She is trying to teach Weiya her trade while the hawk girl's own mother cares for her younger siblings. Weiya proudly claims that the pair are Wakuwai, Ornivians with hawk like features, of the Cloudstalker tribe. As Weiya puts it, her people have hunted in the vast Northern Plains for hundreds of years, hunting the constantly migrating herds that pass through. The girls, in turn, tell the Wakuwai that they are all orphans seeking better lives far from the Blood War, a rehearsed story but not an entirely untrue one.

Lolani and Weiya don't seem concerned at all about Danahlia being a Cold Blood, Twinkaleni being a mage, or even Kaliska being a healer. In fact, they seem pleased to have such a diverse group, believing it will only benefit their chances of successful hunting. Talk doesn't last long, as no one wants to waste sunlight. They discuss some basic tactics and the moment a plan is set, the feathered pair take to the air.

Once out of earshot, Danahlia asks, "What do you guys think?"

"We should try to be friends with them. It's what Althea would want," assures Kaliska.

Twinkaleni and Alice prefer cooperation as well, though Twinkaleni advises caution. Danahlia is eventually convinced of the wisdom in this, if only it means getting more meat.

Alice waits with Kaliska and Squiggles, but with the others working together, it isn't long before they bring down one of the long legged deer Lolani calls an antelope. They divvy it up quickly, the Wakuwai taking their portions along with their empty water gourds before flying off, saying they'll be back tomorrow. Despite their hunger, the girls decide to head toward one of the massive trees that dot the landscape, having learned their lesson from last night.

The trees of the Northern Plains grow straight up and are far taller than they are wide. Fortunately they have thick branches over the majority of the trunk, which the girls intend to use to keep off the ground. The one the girls find that afternoon also has a few fallen branches around it, making a fire much easier for them. Alice carefully chops one of these into more manageable pieces. The branch looks to have fallen ages ago, its bark long gone exposing the pale, dry, brittle wood underneath. Twinkaleni gathers the bits of wood and drops them into the new fire pit they'd dug while Danahlia butchers the animal, Squiggles frequently interrupting for morsels.

Between the crack and snap of old wood, Alice hears something. She looks up, angling her triangular fox ears.

Twinkaleni notices and asks, "What is it?"

Alice holds a finger for silence and the Murin perks up her own abnormally large, round ears. After a few seconds, Alice hears it again, a muted burst of noise. She begins to scan the open plans around them.

Danahlia, noticing the lack of activity, asks, "What?"

Alice shushes her and they all listen while looking around. The sound comes again, closer. Alice feels a hot shiver of dread as she is sure it sounds like Kaliska crying for help. She pans the landscape, her ears pointing all around as she tries to pick up the direction the cries are coming from. Then she spots the Chitali, some distance away, bounding at full speed towards them.

"There!" she points.

They watch for a moment, confused, as Kaliska flies toward them crying breathlessly again and again for help. Then they see something is behind her, mostly concealed by the grass and the deer girl's own body but moving just as swiftly.

"There's somethin' chasin' 'er!" Alice shouts, scrambling for her bow and arrows.

Danahlia takes up her spear and starts to run toward Kaliska while Alice and Twinkaleni wait for an opening. Kaliska runs straight for them, greatly obscuring whatever is after her.

"I can't get a shot!" cries Alice, an arrow drawn to her cheek.

"Nor I, perhaps... asendiote!" calls Twinkaleni with a raise of her tiny, pink hand.

Kaliska begins to float into the air, still trying to flee, and the girls get a glimpse of the feral after her.

It's a large, powerful looking feline of some kind. Its coat is the color of dead grass, letting it blend well with much of the dry plains. With amazing agility, the beast jumps after Kaliska, a reaching clawed paw just grazing her hoof as the beast's momentum carries it flying right into a surprised Danahlia, causing both to tumble to the ground.

The startled feline leaps away from the Liguna then looks after the floating deer girl, confused. It scans around and when it spots Twinkaleni, it immediately charges after her. Alice redraws her bow but, afraid she might hit Danahlia somewhere in the grass, she hesitates, leaving the small Murin open. Alice reaches for her sword but empty air reminds her that she left it by the branch she had been chopping. Too late now to redraw her bow, Alice looks on in horror as the large cat leaps again, its claws out, demanding retribution for its stolen supper.

Time slows for Alice. She shouts warning to the Murin, her injured leg making her far too sluggish to save her this time, though it doesn't stop her from trying.

Twinkaleni uses her other hand, currently not occupied with floating Kaliska, to press down on the grass, with a panicked cry of, "Gravitus!"

The large cat falls mid leap directly to the ground as if rejected by the air itself. But it lands on its feet, inches from the mouse mage. The feline's powerful legs remain bent under it, fighting the gravity Twinkaleni imposes upon it with her earth magic. The ferocious cat displays incredible strength by still managing to get a claw free, raking it across the small girl's face. Twinkaleni squeaks sharply in pain, falling to the grass. The feral beast is freed from her magic and quickly maneuvers over the Murin to finish her. Alice screams, limping and knowing she'll never reach her in time. The monstrous cat beast opens its thick jaw, revealing long, sharp teeth as it reaches for the mage's throat.

Twinkaleni shouts something in terror, her hands raised before her in a final pitiful defense. The cat beast yowls in agony, it's back arching, and nearly doubles over. Twinkaleni shouts again, her voice stronger and less panicked. The powerful cat yowls again, a harsh, frightening cry, its body contorting awkwardly before it tries to limp away, suddenly no longer interested in the hunt. Twinkaleni rises to her feet just as Alice reaches her, nearly falling from the pain in her knee. The Murin's left cheek is a mess of torn flesh and blood, staining her usually pristine, light gray fur, but her amber eyes glow bright gold with a malice Alice can feel in the air around her. The mere sight of them conjures a sensation of such deep dread in the Tokala that she freezes in place.

Twinkaleni doesn't even seem to notice the fox girl, her furiously, glowing eyes targeting the cat creature still struggling to flee. The mage extends her hands out to the beast and thunders in a voice Alice had only heard once before, "SIPHVITAE!"

The monstrous cat yowls horrendously again, curling in on itself as it falls.

The sheer volume of pain reverberating from so fearsome a creature makes Alice scream to the mage, "Stop it!"

Twinkaleni doesn't acknowledge in any way that she hears her. As the mage's splayed fingers curl into cruel claws, the feral's cry stretches out, reaching a pitch so high Alice is forced to pull down her ears and tightly shut her eyes, unable to take it any longer. At its horrible peak, the cry abruptly, wetly, ends.

Chapter 7

Ornivians

Shaking, Alice slowly opens her eyes, but doesn't yet uncover her ears, the terrible noise still echoing in her mind. She sees only the lifeless upper curves of the large cat's body, the rest hidden in the grass. She looks back to Twinkaleni. The Murin's eyes have dimmed to their usual shade and her body sags in exhaustion. A small pink hand reaches up to her torn cheek and she seems surprised to find blood there.

The strange charge in the air has diminished and Alice kneels beside the deeply breathing Murin, only half her own size, "Are you ok?"

Twinkaleni starts, looking at Alice, then back at the blood on her hand, "I, appear to have, been..." She topples over. Alice catches her and lays her down shouting for Kaliska.

Danahlia emerges from the grass with the Chitali, who was dropped from fairly high up when Twinkaleni focused her magic on the cat beast but seems unharmed by it. They hurry over.

"Ticks and fleas! What happened? How'd she

do that?" asks Danahlia, holding a bloody wound at her side, her arm also bleeding from a few claw marks on her bicep.

"I don't know, I think it was some kind o' magic. Are you ok?" Alice asks.

"Yeah, fine," the lizard girl answers, sounding more frustrated with her wounds than hurt by them.

Kaliska sits with her legs crossed beside Twinkaleni, clapping and rubbing her hands together, "That was ugly magic."

"Ugly magic?" Alice asks, tearing her already ragged shirt's sleeve off to wipe at Danahlia's wounds while the Liguna waits to be healed.

Kaliska nods as she leans in to focus on restoring the unconscious Murin's cheek, "Yeah, couldn't you feel it? Real ugly. Full of fear and anger, and suffering."

"Makes sense. Thing almost got 'er," says Danahlia looking over at the cat beast's lifeless form.

Kaliska mmm's as if not entirely agreeing but not wanting to say so as she extends her palms out to the mage. After a few seconds, the torn flesh of Twinkaleni's cheek begins to shift back into place, stretching to cover the four parallel gashes. Blood still stains the mouse girl's fur, but Kaliska seems satisfied and moves on to Danahlia. When she does, Alice wipes Twinkaleni's cheek off to reveal four lines of pink bare but healed flesh. Relieved, Alice limps over to the feral cat's corpse.

The beast is not small, several feet long and, Alice estimates, three hundred pounds or more, much of it looking to be muscle. It's unnaturally twisted as if it had been thrashing in its last moments, its back bent outwardly and limbs splayed. Its coat is coarse and short save for a strip of long brown fur sprouting from the top of its head, extending all the way to the tip of its long tufted tail. It has thickly muscled legs, particularly its hindquarters, and a strong jaw. Crimson drips from much of its face. It's nose, mouth, eyes, and even ears leak, though what draws Alice's attention the most is the pattern they'd made on the ground around it, as if the orifices burst, spraying blood all over.

The Tokala kneels beside the beast, feeling strangely sorry that it came to so violent and painful an end. She jumps a little when Danahlia asks beside her, "Big cat. What happened to its face?"

Alice stands beside the Liguna, giving her head a slight shake, "I don't know. Twinkaleni's magic must've done it."

Danahlia crouches and begins poking around at the very dead feral, "Never saw 'er do that before."

"Her eyes did that thing where they glow," says Alice.

"Yeah, I saw," Danahlia acknowledges.

The only other time they had witnessed this had been back during their struggle with the terrible agent sent by the Order of Thermathrogi to capture or kill the young mage, then again upon discovering the remains of Nesu and the other forest children. Each time, it was frightening to see as much as feel the anger radiating from those eyes, as if the Murin's rage had become a visible, tangible thing.

Alice didn't like to think this way but a tiny thought often nagged her whenever the memory of those glowing eyes drifted through her mind. Twinkaleni's magic had proven time and time again to be a tremendous contributor to the group's survival. But seeing what is did to the small girl, the way it drove her, the way it exhausted her, the way it frustrated her, and then seeing the way she could lose herself in it made Alice wonder if this power was worth its price.

It's late in the evening when the girls take Twinkaleni and the cat beast back to the base of their tree where Squiggles has been busy gluttonously eating the uncooked antelope, completely unaware of the previous events. After laying Twinkaleni down, they gather chopped wood and dried grass for their fire, then convince Squiggles to set it alight. While the remaining antelope cooks, Alice notices Kaliska having great difficultly staying awake. Not wanting to risk another encounter with the night stalking predators of the plains, Alice and Danahlia work together to get the worn out Chitali up into the tree's lower branches.

Once done with that chore, Alice and Danahlia sit before the fire, leaning into each other as they watch their dinner cook.

Alice runs her fingers over the claw marks Kaliska had healed on the Liguna's arm, only slightly paler but smooth skin there now, "I'm worried about Twinkaleni."

Danahlia adjusts the antelope meat over the

crackling fire with a bit of wood as she assures Alice, "She'll be fine, already patched up, just pooped herself out."

Alice gives the lizard girl's arm a squeeze, "That's not what I mean. That spell she used. Kali was right, it *was* ugly magic."

Danahlia rubs a foot under Alice's, "Yeah, that was a new one. But what else could she do? Can't use too much fire out here with all this dry grass, could set the whole plain on fire."

Alice returns the affectionate touch, "I was thinkin', maybe if we relied less on her magic, she wouldn't have to use it so much."

Danahlia stiffen, "You sayin' I don't pull my weight?"

Alice bounces her head off the Liguna's shoulder a few times, "No. I'm sayin' maybe if we did more on our own, Twinkaleni wouldn't feel so pressured to always... improve, her magic as much."

Danahlia nods, "And maybe she won't get all glowy eyed again."

Alice rests her head on the Liguna,

remembering the horrible feeling that coursed through the air, pierced her flesh, and dug into her very soul when she saw the malevolence in the mage's golden eyes.

After sleeping in the safety of the giant tree's branches, the girls have their breakfast and prepare to depart in the direction the Ornivians had said a stream is. Danahlia tries to convince Alice to help her carry the dead feral cat so they have something to eat in case hunting is poor. Not wanting to haul the weight, Alice says to leave it behind, reasoning it would significantly slow them down, making their trek to water all the longer. She doesn't say so but the way it had died also makes her uneasy about even touching it. Twinkaleni offers to float it with her magic, but both girls are quick to shoot down the idea.

Twinkaleni is frowning, saying, "I am much recovered from yesterday. I can at least lighten the beast some as to make it less of a hindrance," when Kaliska points out the Wakuwai pair's return. They once more bring their gourds filled with water, letting the girls and Squiggles drink, then even fill a couple of their waterskins. They're eager to get an early start on the day's hunting, explaining that they had similar hopes to Danahlia in chasing the herd closer to the stream, where they had made camp.

This way they wouldn't need to fly so far each day.

They are surprised to see the slain feral cat. Lolani is especially impressed with this show of the girl's hunting prowess. She tells them that the kasar are one of the most feared predators in the plains and that her people tend to avoid the ground when they see one on the prowl, the large cats' ability to leap making them dangerous even to the feathered hunters. Weiya, on the other hand, is convinced the girls had merely found the cat already dead and claimed it as their own.

The girls offer to share it with the bird folk, who are delighted to have more meat without the need for a hunt. While expertly skinning and butchering the animal into more manageable chunks, Lolani explains that her people believe eating the meat of a kasar grants strength and courage. Killing one of the fearsome beasts is also an important rite of passage for the warriors of her tribe. She smirks as she says the girls would be considered brave indeed for having managed such a feat without even the use of wings.

Lolani and Weiya take their portion of the kasar back to their camp while the girls head after them on foot. A while later when the bird folk return, they discuss beginning a new hunt.

Twinkaleni intends to be a part of it though Danahlia is quick to tell her that she should "sit this one out."

"You may need me if you still intend to bring down another bison," the small mage points out and then asks Alice, "Are you sure you've recovered enough for such a task?"

"Yeah, good as new thanks to Kali," Alice lies, trying desperately not to show a limp in her step.

The Murin looks to Kaliska as if to confirm this but the deer girl just shrugs.

Danahlia sidles up beside Twinkaleni, leaning in to say, "We think it would be best if you kept an eye on Kali."

"Or two," says Kaliska, affectionately looking down at Squiggles squiggling beside her.

Danahlia raises a brow to the Chitali, "Uh, yeah. Make sure she doesn't get into any more trouble, ya know?"

"Very well," Twinkaleni concurs after a moment of thought, adding, "Perhaps then, you should limit your targets to the smaller ferals."

The hunters agree to this and over the course of several days, Danahlia and Alice hunt with the Ornivians, sharing any meat they manage to get, while Twinkaleni and Kaliska follow a safe distance away with Squiggles and much of their belongings.

The hunting is done in a way that continually drives the herd onward in the direction of the stream. Lolani says the herds head there on their own, even if not harried by hunters, as doing so is part of their annual migration. She says the ferals travel continuously, making a massive loop that rings nearly the entirety of the Northern Plains in a ceaseless search for food. The grass here was already dying but the stream's water would keep some green for them. There wouldn't be enough to sustain so many for long however, so the herds will have to move on further northwest to where the moisture trapped by the Gadara Mountains would keep the plain green for a little longer. Then, with winter coming, the herds would start heading back south to warmer climates and would not be seen again this far north until fall of the next year. This meant the Cloudstalker tribe had a limited window of opportunity in which to gather as much meat for the winter as they can, now that it was in abundance.

As they work together, they learn each other's

hunting techniques and come up with some new strategies to help insure successful hunts. One that works fairly well on the smaller beasts has Weiya or, more successfully, Lolani swoop down on to a feral's back while entangling their heads with the partially repaired net. The Ornivian would then pull back on the net from the rear, forcing the beast to expose its neck to a slash or stab from in front by the earthbound hunters. Even then it could be dangerous, many of the herd's members having horns and all having powerful legs equipped with hard hooves.

After a good strike, the hunters would retreat from the stricken feral until it succumbed to its wounds. Both parties prefer a quick death for their prey and do their best to be precise as a show of respect and to honor the feral's sacrifice. Danahlia makes most of the handful of kills though once Alice's leg has healed enough, with Kaliska's help, the Tokala manages to contribute as well. The Wakuwai are overjoyed with the hunts' successes and return everyday with water for the girls and the hopes of more meat.

As the party nears the stream, they notice the trees they try to camp in at night are getting larger and more frequent, some towering so high they look like they might brush the passing clouds. The trunks also swell with the trees' height, some taking minutes just to pass around. Lolani, who takes pleasure in sharing the knowledge and ways of her people, says the massive trees are called, Zalonya, or "mountain fingers" if loosely translated into the common tongue of Arsalia. They are believed by her people to be the fingers of the mountain gods that have sprung up from the earth to hold up the sky, allowing all life to exist between them. As such, the Zalonya trees are considered sacred and none have ever been cut down by the Cloudstalkers.

The girls rejoice when they finally see the lush, green grasses and thick gatherings of ferals that must mean they've finally reached the stream. They run to it whooping and hooting, parting a sea of startled beasts until their feet squish through mud and finally patter into the cool water. It had been weeks since they'd had access to so much and they take full advantage of it, splashing each other happily. The wary ferals look on but their thirst after so long a march through the dry plains keeps them nearby.

The stream is shallow, not even a foot deep in most places, but at least several yards wide. The water is muddy though kept cool even in the sun thanks to the fall temperatures. After a bit of play, the Ornivians appear, gliding down to the stream to greet the girls, pleased they had finally made it. They point out their camp, further upstream and high in a Zalonya tree, inviting Alice and her friends to visit. The Cloudstalkers quickly depart saying they are very busy preparing all the meat the girls had helped hunt.

Alone once more, the girls bathe and do what they can to clean their ragged, dirty clothes. Weiya reappears, bringing with her something Alice had not seen in a long while. Soap. The young Cloudstalker had made comments about the girl's smell as they hunted and now seems intent on doing something about it. She breaks her offering into a few chunks and with them the girls can finally get in a proper cleaning. The soap is light gray in color, slightly darker than Twinkaleni's fur, but smells pleasantly of wild flowers.

Weiya sticks around as if to insure they know how to use soap, allowing Alice to ask where she came by it. The Wakuwai girl rather proudly says she made it herself using techniques passed down by her people. As the girls wash, Weiya recounts the many labors involved with making the soap, from the collecting of ash, to rending fat, all the way to extracting oil from flowers. She smiles when she receives compliments on her product, mostly from Kaliska who has taken a liking to blowing bubbles with it to Squiggles, the young dragon splashing about popping them.

After they've cleaned as much as they can, Weiya leaves them once more to dry. Alice, Danahlia, and Kaliska lay spread eagle in the grass without shame, but Twinkaleni uses this as an opportunity to test her water siphon spell on herself. Doing so, she manages to get her fur dry within a very short time. Pleased with her success, she moves on to dry the girl's clothes as well. Watching Kaliska role around in the grass, pulling up bits to munch on, gets Alice thinking about food.

The girls decide to make camp in the tree the Ornivians have, though the bird people are settled much higher in it than the mostly wingless party could manage to climb even if they tried. Upon reaching the base of the truly massive tree, Lolani and Weiya descend to offer them a few select pieces of meat dried into jerky, the valued end product of all their hunting. The girls accept the gift gratefully and invite the Ornivians to dine with them in celebration of their reaching the stream, successful hunts, and new friendship.

Alice sniffs at the jerky hanging from a bit of grass woven rope, finding it has the strong scent of unfamiliar spices. Never one to shy from trying new meats, Danahlia begins to chew on hers as Lolani explains that these pieces are from one of the Wakuwai pair's earlier hunts here by the stream. She says that the powerful aroma is from the cayie pepper's seeds, which are crushed into a powder and spread over the meat. The cayie pepper, along with its seeds, are exceptionally hot and are commonly used by her people to keep meat fresher for longer, as well as to help cover the taste of spoiling meat in leaner times. It's when the hawk woman is telling them this that Danahlia suddenly sprints to the stream to dunk her head in the water, making Weiya burst into high-pitched, squawking laughter.

The girls produce a good deal of meat from their stores and both groups feast together well into the night. Eventually, after Danahlia's pestering and then even having her courage questioned, Alice does try the cayie seasoned jerky. She finds it has a nice chewy texture and an interesting flavor, though this is buried *deep* under the tongue searing, nostril burning heat of the spice. Squiggles manages to get hold of some and eats it readily, apparently immune or swallowing too quickly for the spice to take affect. Twinkaleni tries some too and Alice finds it amusing to watch the Murin attempt to maintain her composure despite her eyes watering profusely.

Over the next few weeks, the girls hunt frequently with the Ornivians and with each passing day they become more and more certain they made the right decision in cooperating with them. Game is easy to find for a time and with the Wakuwai freely sharing their knowledge of meat drying and rope making, the girls learn how to make their own jerky. They hang it from the most sun exposed branches, high enough so that predators won't get to it. The near constant breeze helps dry the meat though it still takes many days for the raw meat to become good jerky.

The girls share a rehearsed but not entirely untrue story of why they have come to the Northern Plains and intend to continue into the Gadara Mountains. Danahlia is one of the many Cold Bloods that was trapped in Warm Blood territory once the current Blood War began. While in hiding, she met Alice and Twinkaleni, both war orphans. The three decided, for the Liguna's safety, to make for the mountainous north, known to be the least populated region of Arsalia, in the hopes of escaping the war and all the hardship it had already brought them. Along the way they met Kaliska, a wandering healer, and eventually picked up Squiggles.

Lolani shows no hostility toward Danahlia for being cold blooded. Weiya, by contrast, is eager to challenge Danahlia in various tasks and shows of skill, though Alice finds this is due to the two girls' clashing competitive natures rather than any racial animosity. The bird woman says that her people have never had reason to dislike the Cold Bloods and only take part in the wars because of pressure put on them by the terrestrial Warm Bloods, or *furred ones,* as she refers to Alice, Twinkaleni, and Kaliska's kind.

She seems more irate with Arsalia than Feoria, the loose conglomerate of territories that make up the Cold Blood's country, for the troubles brought on her tribe. She says it's because of the furred ones that many of their people, men mostly but also women, are taken to serve Arsalia in this time of war. This, she says hotly, has left "fewer skilled talons to feed many hungry beaks."
This seems to be a common theme wherever Alice and her friends go but she has to ask why women were also taken. Lolani explains that the number "recruited" from each tribe is related to the tribes' size, and since they're expected to serve as message carriers and scouts rather than warriors, the earthbound Arsalians are more interested in acquiring the fastest fliers than being picky about gender. Lolani's words are heated but she says she does not blame the girls in the least, knowing they have nothing to do with such matters.

A few days after the girls arrive at the stream, they spot some other Wakuwai flying to Lolani and Weiya's tree. Most seem smaller than Weiya and peer curiously at Alice's party but don't come down. After loading their talons with jerky and other items from the tree top camp, they quickly depart, heading back north. Weiya flies down and informs the girls that they were other members of her tribe. Too young to hunt yet, they help by taking supplies from the hunter's camps back to where the majority of their tribe is roosting in the mountains. From then, Alice notices they come once every week or so.

Aside from drying the meat, the Ornivians use many other parts of the animals they hunt. They dry and clean the skins for various things, including clothing and insulation for their homes. Bones are used to make tools, weapons, and sometimes jewelry. Hooves can be made into glue and even various organs, such as the bladder and stomach, are used as containers for transporting water and other liquids. Only the first part of the processes are done here by Lolani and Weiya, just enough so that the younger Cloudstalkers can take the bundles of rolled skins and other things back with them to the tribe's main encampment.

Seeing how much effort the Ornivians put in to making use of as much of their prey as possible makes Alice feel a bit guilty about how she and her friends generally just pick off the meat they want and let the rest go to waste. She tries not to dwell though, instead using it to fuel her eagerness to learn.

Generally after a successful hunt, the rest of the day will be spent preparing their quarry's various bits for transport. This means carefully removing the hide with surprisingly effective bone bladed knives. The goal is to get the skin off in one piece, which takes an experienced hand. The hide is then laid out on a rock or other flat surface and scraped free off excess flesh and fat. These rawhides are then tied into bundles along with other useful animal products and set to await pick up the next time the young transport team stops by.

To make the jerky, the meat of an animal is cut into the thinnest, longest, strips possible. Weiya is particularly adept at this and is eager to show off her skill to the others. Any fat is removed because it causes spoilage during drying, but is saved, as it can be used to make other things including something they call pemmican. They learn pemmican is a food made by jerky that is so dry it becomes brittle. This jerky is then crushed into a powder and mixed with heated fat as well as berries, seeds, and herbs for added flavor. It's then set to cool and harden, becoming a meal that can be preserved for an extended period of time. It doesn't sound particularly appetizing to Alice but Weiya insists it is good stewed and that the girls will be thankful for it during winter.

After many hunts, the herds eat nearly all of the green grass by the stream. The ferals then begin moving northeast in search of more, as Lolani had said they would, making hunting trips longer by the day. The stream also steadily dries along with what's left of the grass, its distant mountain source freezes in the face of the oncoming winter. While the Cloudstalkers prepare to leave their hunting post, they invite Alice's party to their main camp deep in the mountains. Lolani assures them that they will be warmly welcomed and the girls, having no other real plans, decide to take them up on the offer.

They follow the stream north as they are told to, keeping ahead of its drying so they have a source of water. The Zalonya trees are evergreens and remain vibrant even as the rest of the landscape yellows and browns. There are more of them the further the girls travel, which is nice for Kaliska. She's taken a liking to their short flexible needle like leaves and claims they are sweet and tangy. The others take her word for it, having plenty of meat from their hunts to last them for some time.

The party passes the occasional small village or possibly large camp, keeping their distance as Twinkaleni had advised them to do after leaving the Great Horn. The people who make this land their home look to be hunters and herdsman for the most part. Every now and again, Lolani and Weiya will find them and encourage them to keep on course, seeming very interested in getting the girls to visit their home. Even so, it is many days before the party can make out the impressive viridian forests at the foot of the snow topped Gadara Mountain range.

As the days pass, Squiggles grows quickly, already the size of a large dog, and his appetite grows to match. What looked like enough meat to last weeks is already nearly gone and the girls must try to hunt again. Squiggles himself proves to be a clumsy hunter at best. He's grown too large for the girls to maintain much control over and whenever he sees some beast he wishes to prey on, he immediately races off after it. His prey often hears his noisy approach and are off before he gets anywhere near them, though this doesn't stop the young dragon from using his fiery breath, which so far has only resulted in the girls needing to run after him to beat out the fires he starts before the whole of the north is set ablaze.

The further they travel, the colder it becomes as well. Alice, Twinkaleni, and Kaliska's fur coats thicken for the cooler weather, but Danahlia is left holding some of the rawhides they'd gotten from their hunts about herself to keep warm. She insists she's fine but more and more often through chattering teeth. Squiggles, too, seems more sluggish and tires quickly. After some discussion, the party decides they'll need to stop at the next village for provisions and some warmer clothes.

In the late afternoon of the next day, the party comes across a small huddle of buildings surrounded by fenced enclosures. Judging by the squat sheep like creatures with long, floppy ears within them, they deduce that they're animal pens. The girls keep their distance, luring Squiggles away before he spots them. They agree that Alice and Kaliska are the least conspicuous and will enter the village to barter. The party has little but hands over what they don't immediately need to the pair so they might have better luck trading. Twinkaleni hands Alice her book, a combination bestiary and herbiary. The large tome had helped them countless times in identifying the various animals and plants they had come across, letting them know what was safe or not to eat or what ferals were too dangerous to hunt.

"Twinkaleni, I can't take this," Alice says, knowing how much the book means to the small Murin.

Alice tries to give it back but the mage refuses it, "Of course you can. It is quite possibly the most valuable thing we own, and we cannot afford to be sentimental."

Alice frowns, looking down at the book's blank green cover and recalling the many evenings they had spent looking at all the intricately detailed drawings contained within its pages.

"It is of no concern." Twinkaleni assures, "I have committed the entirety of its contents to memory. Besides, I've become rather tired of carrying it, it's... rather heavy, and bulky," shes says, her voice breaking a little as she eyes it. The mage then looks away, "Just be sure you bring back its worth."

Alice nods and places the book in her pack with the various other things they will try to barter with.

Chapter 8

Drakoda

Alice and Kaliska do not enter the village until night. They use the darkness to approach in secret, keeping away from the animal pens. Or at least Alice does. As the fox girl creeps closer to the houses, she hears the curious calls of the animals confined to the enclosures. Looking back, she spots Kaliska leaning over the short wooden fences separating her from the animals with her hands held out to them. The creatures approach her, sniffing, as some in the back *baa* warily. Alice hurries back to the Chitali, grabbing her by the shoulder and spinning her around to face her.

"What are you doing?! We're supposed to be sneaking!" she whispers as harshly and quietly as she can.

Kaliska frowns at her tone, "They were lonely. I just wanted to say, hi."

Alice's response catches in her throat as several things try to come out at once. Instead she just grabs the deer girl by the forearm and drags her away from the animals, now *baa*-ing more urgently.

As they near the first house, Alice crouches and tugs on the still held Chitali's forearm, getting her to do the same. Alice then reaches around the fence post nearest the gate and feels for the marks as Twinkaleni had taught her to do back in Carton. As the pair moves from post to post and house to house, Alice notices Kaliska hugging fence posts. The fox girl is shaking her head in disbelief as Kaliska squats beside her and hugs the post next to the one Alice had just checked.

"Why are you doing that?" Alice whispers.

"You were doin' it. I give good hugs. Want one?" Kaliska asks opening her arms to Alice.

Alice briefly considers taking the Chitali back and getting one of the others but reminds herself that as they discussed, Danahlia would be too easily recognized and Twinkaleni's large ears made her easy to remember, plus her small size meant she couldn't carry as much without using magic.

Alice takes the deer girl's hands and presses them together, "No, I don't. Just follow me, ok?"

They check much of the village but find no sign of the marks, positive or negative, and simply wait until morning before a small shop. The shop is dug into a modest mound of earth but has a door with a sign over it and even a window. When the keeper comes to open, the elderly, almost completely white furred Murin man seems surprised to even have customers. He eyes the pair suspiciously from behind large, round spectacles as they explain their needs. After nodding along with the girls he leads them into his shop.

Inside, he looks over what the girls have to trade with: a few coins of little value, a knife, some skins, a few bones, teeth, and horns Danahlia thought looked interesting, and one last large emberstone Twinkaleni had been saving. After much beard stroking, the Murin says the girls will have to get meat from the herdsmen but he does have a stock of thick coats made from the floppy eared, sheep beasts' wool, though what they've shown him will not be enough for all they need.

Alice hadn't wanted to, but she pulls free Twinkaleni's book from her pack and sets it on the Murin's short counter top, now nearly taking up the whole of it. Alice can tell he is very interested as he begins to flip through the pages, adjusting his glasses, and looking over the masterful artwork with its detailed descriptions. He stops to read an entry but Alice closes the book before he can get too far and eventually arranges a deal. The book and the emberstone for four thick, well-made, wooly coats and an assortment of other garments.

Trying on her new coat, Alice loads up Kaliska with all the rest and has her wait as the fox girl heads into a fenced pasture with many woolly beasts and a young, light furred Caprican looking after them. When Alice inquires about procuring meat, the goat boy leads her to a small wooden shed. Inside is the boy's father in the middle of butchering one of his stock for a large, patiently waiting, female Urock. The Caprican man leans heavily against a thick wooden table, his right leg ending at the knee with a crutch nearby. He listens to Alice's proposal as he prepares the bear woman's order.

He seems pleased with the arrangement, commenting that the bear woman hadn't wanted the whole animal, and agrees to trade with Alice for the rest. He takes the skins, knife, coins, and his son seems to like the teeth and horns Danahlia had collected, so he takes those too, giving Alice a fair supply of raw meat. Alice heads back to find the clothes she had just traded for in a pile by the fence. Kaliska is standing within the enclosure, surrounded by the wooly ferals, and singing as the Caprican boy looks on in amusement. The Chitali baas musically and many of the ferals respond.

Alice smiles and waves, "Kali, it's time to go."

"Oh, Alice, listen to them. They're singing!" Kaliska calls back, gesturing grandly at the poofy beasts moving around her in a confused mob.

It takes a little more coaxing but Alice manages to get Kaliska to leave the beasts and the pair walks back to their friends, Kaliska singing baas the whole way.

"Hey, not bad," Danahlia exclaims, putting on her new wool coat.

Alice smiles at her, but then falls into the Liguna when Squiggles jumps on her from behind, trying to get into her meat ladened backpack.

They both shout, "No!" and wave the dragon away. Squiggles makes disappointed noises and tries his luck with Kaliska.

Danahlia holds Alice against her chest, "Mmm, you're warm."

"He's hungry," says Kaliska, rubbing noses with Squiggles.

"He's *always* hungry," replies Alice, pulling Danahlia's coat flaps around her so they can share their warmth.

"Indeed," comments Twinkaleni, tying a bit of grass woven rope around her like a belt so her own coat doesn't drag so far behind her, "But we must continue with rationing in mind. It may be sometime before we can procure additional resources and we have little to trade with."

Set in their new garments, the party continues on, the sky scraping peaks of the Gadara Mountains looming ever closer. Danahlia and Alice get Twinkaleni and Kaliska to train with them in mock battles to better prepare for their uncertain future and encourage the Murin mage to rely on her modest physical skills more and her magic less. Twinkaleni agrees to this, adding that the overt use of magic is an unnecessary risk. Even so, she does not shy away from cleverly using a sudden burst of air here and a little gravity manipulation there to give herself an edge. These duels rarely last more than a minute as Squiggles becomes rather fond of stripping the combatants of their fighting sticks and quickly chewing them to splinters.

Twinkaleni also doesn't hesitate to use her magic to hunt. She uses a new spell, one similar to the one used against the large, predatory, cat beast Lolani had called a kasar. It's a strange thing to witness. Upon spotting a feral, Twinkaleni will raise a hand to it, her fingers slowly closing as if around a small fruit. After a few moments, if the creature remains still enough, she will whisper, "Siphvitae," suddenly squeezing her hand closed. The beast will simply drop, most dying instantly. There is no fiery bolt cast, no visible gathering or release of energies, or any great show of magical forces at all. It's almost frightening in its transparency.

Twinkaleni explains it as "a logical evolution" of her water siphoning spell. As she could manipulate and pull free water from plants, she can now do similarly to the blood in living beings. She says she began to feel it in her companions as she was reaching out to the grasses in the plains just as she did the moisture in plants. It was only a matter of capturing it. She says this is considerably more difficult, as the blood inside of creatures is constantly moving and changing so rapidly. But after her "success" with the kasar, which she admits was "unrefined," she has become interested in applying the theory more practically. Surrounded by furrowed brows, Twinkaleni says that the spell allows her to manipulate a creature's blood to some degree and causes it to collect and rupture parts of the brain.

"That's bad magic, Twinkles. You shouldn't use that," affirms Kaliska.

"Yeah, that sounds kinda evil," says Alice, recalling that only the most vile witches and sorcerers used such spells in stories.

Danahlia nods her agreement but Twinkaleni scoffs defensively, crossing her arms over her tiny chest, "Nonsense. There is no 'evil' magic. There is only energy and the will to employ it. And why shouldn't I use it? Would it be preferable to burn a feral alive with a firebolt? Or," she narrows her eyes at Alice, "To pierce a creature with arrows until its pain causes it to collapse only to have its throat slit?" Twinkaleni raises her chin, walking on, "My spell causes near instant death when properly employed, minimizing our risk as well as any suffering on the part of our quarry."

The others find this difficult to argue against but Danahlia insists the Murin not use her new spell so often that Alice and herself can't get any needed hunting practice in. So far, the mage can use it successfully only on smaller birds and rodents but clearly has aspirations to develop it further. She insists that it will be of great value to them and proves it by insuring Squiggles has plenty of snacks.

The Murin uses her new spell freely, and is very proud of it, though Alice, Danahlia, and especially Kaliska, do not share her enthusiasm.

Their journey continues with Lolani and Weiya visiting more regularly, saying the girls are getting closer and closer to their winter camp. They've traded in their loose hunting garments for longer and no doubt warmer garb. As they near their feathered friend's temporary home, a few younger Cloudstalkers accompany the pair but keep their distance high in the trees, both wary and curious about the party of outsiders. Lolani says that furred ones are few this far north and many are not friendly toward her people. Bare ones like Danahlia are even rarer and everyone in the Cloudstalker tribe is eagerly awaiting their arrival. Some, she says waving a wing at the younger members, were too impatient to wait.

Alice can hear the younger ones talking among themselves. They speak in a language she isn't familiar with but one word is uttered enough to peek her curiosity and she asks Weiya what it means.

The hawk girl says, "Drakoda, means dragon friend."

Twinkaleni tries to argue that Squiggles is not a dragon but Weiya just grins and says her people seem to have heard otherwise.

The zalonya trees become thicker and thicker as the girls enter in earnest the vast forest at the foot of the Gadara Mountains, and as the trees become more numerous so to do the Cloudstalker visitors. Lolani and Weiya are always among them and have been bringing pieces of jerky and other food for the girls as well as for Squiggles. It takes time but eventually the dragon begins to greet the bird people excitedly, knowing there will be some interesting treats in it for him. Alice feels a bit guilty for accepting so much hospitality, knowing her and her friends had little to offer in return, but Lolani says her kin insist on it. She says it has been a very long time since both dragon and drakoda have been seen by her people and that they should expect even more such treatment to come.

Visits from the Wakuwai become a near daily event. Mostly children come but a few adults do as well, and all are particularly interested in Squiggles. They bring him offerings of food and rocks, delighting in watching him eat them. With the frequent meals, the young dragon continues to grow bigger and stronger. His once fairly smooth, supple scales take on a more ridged feel, still flexible but steadily getting tougher. The tiny horns jutting back from his head and the one poking up from his nose also grow longer and harder. Twinkaleni excitedly says that these kinds of growths show he is in good health and well on his way to becoming a powerful Gullveigaryan.

As the girls travel to the Cloudstalker's camp, Squiggles doubles in size again, going from the size of a large dog to that of a juvenile horse. He even lets Twinkaleni ride on his back a little, though it takes trial and error figure out how best to keep the small mage aboard. If he walks slowly enough, Twinkaleni can generally keep atop him, but any faster and she ends up sliding off, her legs too short to give her much of a hold. Thankfully, Squiggles can feel the Murin slipping and stops whenever she does, keeping her from being trampled and allowing one of the others, keeping pace, to catch her, most of the time. Still, Twinkaleni keeps at it, insisting that according to her reading, dragons must be trained from their youth to follow commands or else there is great risk of them becoming too independent and thus, uncontrollable. Eventually, with the help of a few well-placed grass woven straps, Twinkaleni can ride atop Squiggles while maintaining a respectable pace. And though she tries to retain an air of seriousness about the training, Alice can tell Twinkaleni is enjoying herself.

One day, already escorted by several Ornivians, sharp cries alert the girls to dozens of the bird people gliding down from the trees. Alice had seen a few of them before on their way in and these come forth to greet them while the others look on with undisguised interest. The unfamiliar ones, mostly older adults, seem particularly impressed when their kin are able to pet Squiggles and the word, Drakoda, is spoken many times.

Alice tries to endure but is made uncomfortable by all the attention and by the look of it, so are Twinkaleni and Danahlia, though Kaliska, by contrast, is enjoying her following of the younger Ornivians, many roughly Twinkaleni's size. Aside from Squiggles, other youths take a particular liking to Kaliska, Twinkaleni, and Alice's ears, giggling whenever they angle at various sounds they make. The bird folk, themselves, lack visible ears but clearly have no trouble hearing when Lolani calls out to settle them down.

The girls regroup and Danahlia nudges Alice with an elbow, "Didn't think there'd be so many."

"I know," Alice replies, "At least they're happy to see us."

Twinkaleni reminds, "We should put every effort into maintaining good relations with these people. They will likely be vital to our surviving the winter here."

The girls are led to a clearing in a ring of exceptionally thick zalonya trees and several adult Cloudstalkers glide down before them to lay thick, long loops of braided vines at their feet. Uncertain of what is expected of them, Alice asks what they're for.

Lolani points to the loops, then straight up, "You sit, hold tight. We fly you up. Ulima, our (she says a word Alice doesn't understand), been waiting for you."

The girls follow the gesture. Especially high up in the thick branches of the mighty Zalonya trees, Alice can make out what appear to be large, mud colored platforms. They look somewhat like Lolani and Weiya's stream side camp from below and Alice assumes they must be the tribe's dwellings.

"That is *really* up there," comments Danahlia, bending backwards to see.

Twinkaleni uses a tiny pink foot to prod the braided vine loops, "Are you quite sure these will hold our weight? Have they been tested?"

"No worries," assures Weiya, "You fall, you scream, catch you we will, we will we will."

Looking at the height they will have to reach to get to the platforms, Alice is thinking, *screaming won't be the problem,* when Kaliska says excitedly beside her, "Let's go, let's go!" The Chitali is already sitting on a section of a vine loop, whipping the rest before her like reins.

Three of the adult Ornivians grab hold of Kaliska's loop in their talons and begins flapping their massive wings, taking flight. When the loop becomes taut, Kaliska suddenly jerks into the air after them with a cry that quickly turns to laughter. As Kaliska ascends to cheers of the other Wakuwai, Alice, Danahlia, and Twinkaleni look to each other and then at their waiting loops.

Danahlia takes in a deep breath, "No way Deernuts is braver than me." She sits on a loop as Kaliska had and a few more Ornivians grab hold of it and take to the air. The moment Danahlia is jolted off the ground she cries, "Oh, Tiiicks!"

Alice watches Danahlia being carried off without incident and looks down at the second to last loop, muttering to herself, "No tucking, noo tucking," as she forces her tail out behind her and sits down on a section of the vines.

She grasps them in both hands, feeling their smooth, flexible strength. She takes a few deep breaths before nodding to the trio of Cloudstalkers taking the other end of the loop in their talons. She gets a smile back and the three bird people begin to flap their wings, kicking up dust.

Alice watches the Cloudstalkers take to the air and grips her vines tighter. She grits her teeth and digs her nails into the vines as the loop becomes taut and suddenly she's jerked skyward. Alice immediately slides back and for a second thinks she might slide off, but she hooks her legs so the braided vines catch behind her knees as she climbs into the air. The Ornivians must flap hard to lift her, making for a bumpy start, but once aloft, they find their rhythm and ride becomes considerably smoother, even enjoyable.

As her confidence in the Wakuwai and their vines' strength grows, Alice steadily relaxes, looking down as she's pulled away from the stable, comforting ground into the free and unfamiliar air. The hawk people's wings create gusts that mingle with the wind passing over Alice, making looking up at them a little uncomfortable. But she notices them looking back down at her occasionally while talking excitedly to each other in their unknown tongue. Instead, Alice looks around as they make large circles, slowly ascending. She spots Twinkaleni rising from below. The Murin has opted to lay on her loop and uses both her legs and arms to grip the vines tightly, only two Cloudstalkers needed to carry her.

Alice sees Squiggles too, his dark red skin contrasting sharply with the pale, brown bark of the Zalonya tree he clambers up. He calls to her and Alice shouts back encouragement. The dragon climbs well, using not only his four clawed limbs but also two sharp, hooked digits extending from the main joint on his wings.

After a few minutes of pleasant flight, Danahlia and her Wakuwai come into view above and across from where Alice's team ascends. The Tokala is surprised to see the lizard girl still gripping her vines hard, her taloned feet rigidly tucked under her with even her long tail wrapped around the vines for added assurance.

Alice grins deviously and shouts, "You're not tuckin' over there are ya?!"

Danahlia jerks her head over at the sound and

Alice can see her force clenched teeth apart to yell, "Not a chance, Furface, just enjoyin' the ride!"

Danahlia's Ornivians seem to take this as some sort of cue and begin to flap harder, sending Danahlia cringing up higher and faster. Not to be outdone, Alice's team increase their own pace, racing their tribesmen. Alice cheers them on, bouncing wildly underneath the trio of Cloudstalkers. More bird folk, younger ones especially, join in, showing off their aerial acrobatics and calling encouragingly to the competitors hauling up the girls. Alice can't help but laugh as the wind flows hastily through her fur and she sees Danahlia gripping her vines tighter than ever.

The ride slows as they reach the height of the platform which turns out to be a sort of bulbous structure nestled into the cleft of a zalonya's trunk and a particularly large branch. It looks vaguely like the hornet's nests Alice had seen around the forest near Toki village except it's the size of a small house. It has a large, circular opening that Alice takes to be the entrance along with a few more that must be windows, all covered from the inside by animal skins. Looking around, Alice sees the largest branches of nearby zalonya trees also host similar dwellings, most with smoke pluming from their round but tapering tops, reminding her strangely of onions.

Danahlia plops off her vine loop onto a wide branch that, looking along it, Alice sees must have been intertwined with another in a nearby tree at some point. The two now grow together, forming an impressive living bridge that spans the open air between two Ornivian dwellings. As Alice is set beside the Liguna, she can see there are several more of these bridges crisscrossing between trees with houses of their own. Danahlia belly crawls to the edge of the bridge and peers over. She immediately turns away, not liking what she sees, and looking like she might be sick.

Alice kneels down beside her, patting the larger girl on the back, "It wasn't that bad was it?"

"Bumpy...too, bumpy..." Danahlia croaks in between deep breaths just before her cheeks puff out.

Kaliska appears from somewhere and grabs Alice from behind saying cheerily, "Wasn't that amazing?! Look how high we are!"

Alice does and is immediately hit hard with vertigo, feeling herself lose balance despite most of her weight being safely anchored on the branch bridge. Fortunately, Twinkaleni's Ornivian team soon blocks their view of the distant ground. Danahlia swallows hard as the Murin quickly hops off her vines to join them.

"A most, exhilarating experience," the small mage comments through quick breaths while looking around at their new surroundings.

"Wasn't it great?" asks Kaliska jubilantly, "I wonder if they'll let us ride again."

"We have to get down somehow," Alice grins.

Danahlia groans, clearly not looking forward to it as many of the younger Ornivians land around them, cheering and talking excitedly among themselves. Under the chatter, Alice can hear Squiggles calling in distress. The girls look over the bridge to where the dragon is set, claws dug into the side of the tree, still a ways down. Some of the other Ornivians seem to be encouraging him to try using his wings, but the dragon looks like he's simply too tired to continue the climb.

Those who carried the girls take up their vines once more and head down to him to begin trying to get the loops around the dragon's limbs, tail, and shoulders. It's no easy task for the Cloudstalkers, as

Squiggles doesn't seem interested in releasing his grip from the tree, though he doesn't entirely fight their efforts either. Perhaps because he saw how the bird people had lifted the girls, he eventually lets go his perch once enough vines are secured around him and swings into the air. His weight proves too great. The handful of bird people lose altitude despite their efforts but soon the others of the tribe move in. More talons and wings are added to the task and the dragon slowly begins upward.

It takes several nail biting minutes, but the Cloudstalkers eventually get Squiggles up to the bridge. The moment his claws can touch the entwined branches, he pulls free from the bird folk and rushes for the girls. Still tangled in the vines, Squiggles thrusts his head among them, in great need of comforting words and pets. The Ornivians land all about, exhausted from their efforts, as the girls and the youngest Cloudstalkers cheer their success.

Once the vines are removed and Squiggles settles a bit, Lolani leads the girls to the first dwelling Alice had seen. When they near it, the skin hanging in place of a door is moved aside and an elderly Wakuwai woman appears, wrapped thickly in skins and leaning heavily on a short cane.

"Ulima," says Lolani, "The eldest and wisest of us. Has been looking forward to meeting you."

"Hurry it up, you're lettin' the cold in!" grumbles the diminutive elder in common Arsalian, stepping to the side of her doorway and waving to them impatiently.

The girls look to each other and then follow Lolani in quickening their pace. Up close, Ulima looks frail and withered under her layers of warm clothing. Her feathers are disheveled and small patches are missing in some places along her neck and head, the only areas not covered by hides. She has a few necklaces that look like they may be using teeth as beads, but what stands out the most are the milky blank eyes that only look in the party's general direction. Alice can't help but pause, curious to see if there are pupils in the murky white.

"Yes, I'm blind," grumbles Ulima, startling the fox girl, "It's rude to stare ya know."

Before Alice can apologize, a young Cloudstalker boy waves to them to sit on some round pads around a fire situated in the center of the surprisingly spacious one room dwelling. The other Wakuwai have become quite and wait outside. Not wanting to break the silence, Alice and her friends do as they are bid, ducking to get through the doorway. The fire keeps the dwelling warm and unusual scents and sights make the girls look and sniff around in wonder.

The walls are layered with hides, no doubt to keep the place insulated though some clearly have other purposes, their fur removed and skin elaborately painted with colorful patters, symbols and images of beasts. The floor is similarly covered in furred skins, making it soft and pleasant under foot with only a rough bare circle around the fire. The ceiling is a dome with the highest point opening just over the fire to let the smoke out. Things dangle from it, anchored by intersecting sticks and hanging from woven strands of string. Some are vegetables, dried herbs, and meats, while other unidentifiable objects hang in small sacks.

One, dangling close to Alice, smells particularly pungent and Ulima says from the door way, without quite looking in her direction, "Keeps the bugs away."

Squiggles pokes his head in after the girls and sniffs around, the entrance far too small for him.

Ulima reaches out and rubs his snout, smiling wearily, "Didn't think there were any more o' you left." Squiggles nuzzles into her hand and then snorts. "Oh, I won't keep 'em long. You just wait a minute," the elderly woman says, turning to hobble over to a few pillows by the fire. She plops down on them and hands her cane off to the air. The silent Ornivian boy manages to catch it before it falls over and the old woman grins.

Squiggles keeps his head inside, letting the door skin hang over his neck as he lays down. Some of the younger Cloudstalkers poke their hands into the windows to move aside the curtains so they can peek in as the girls sit on the woven pads, painted with circles of orange, green, and red, looking to the elderly woman expectantly. Ulima just sits with a slight smile, nodding subtly as if agreeing to some unheard conversation.

The girls look to each other and around the dwelling for a few minutes until Ulima finally says, "You're a patient bunch. I like that. First things first, you all want to stick around here for a while. Winters in these mountains can be difficult and no one wants more mouths to feed."

"Lolani said we'd be welcome," interjects Alice, considering the long journey it's taken to get here.

"Lolani doesn't make the decisions here. Not

as long as I still have one talon gripped to this world," counters the withered old woman, "and I must do what's best for my people. It isn't easy having so many looking to you to solve all their problems."

"If they don't want us, we can do just fine on our own," grumbles Danahlia, starting to rise.

Twinkaleni tugs on the much larger girl's coat sleeve and says to Ulima, "We do not expect to be waited on. We are not without skills of our own."

Alice nods, adding, "We can work for our meals, and hunt them ourselves if we need to. We mostly just need a place to stay out o' the cold."

"I can sing," Kaliska offers.

"You can heal," corrects Danahlia.

"Yeah, that too," Kaliska agrees.

Ulima takes this in thoughtfully before replying, "Oh, I know. Young Weiya has said you are decent hunters. Coming from her, it can only be true." She then says toward Danahlia, "Though from what I see, you're also brave, if reckless..." She pans her blind gaze over Alice, "...selfless, if naïve...," she says over Twinkaleni, "...clever, if inexperienced...," then nods to Kaliska, "...and kind, if gullible."

Danahlia frowns but Kaliska smiles brightly, "That's a cute word."

"I beg your pardon, but you said 'see'?" asks Twinkaleni.

Ulima straightens her neck some, "Yes. Even after my sight was taken I could still see the light in folk, and the dark." The aging Wakuwai leans in as if to keep others from hearing. "They all think I'm wise," she says, indicating with a jerk of her head the Cloudstalkers peering silently in through the windows, she then leans back smiling, "But mostly I'm just really old and a good judge of character."

Alice looks to Danahlia, who shrugs, and the fox girl asks, "So, may we stay in your village?"

Ulima begins to rock back and forth like a bored child might while she thinks toward the ceiling, "Mmm, we do have a few empty nests... and you did help us in the plains. Food is always an issue during winter, but you got some huntin' skills..." Ulima trails off and considers for a few moments until Squiggles snorts, clearly feeling this is taking too long. The Cloudstalker elder gives him a side smile, "And the dragon seems to like you... so yeah, you can stay awhile."

The girls cheer among themselves, elated that they might finally have a place to stay for a time. Word spreads from the Cloudstalkers at the window to those waiting behind them and loud cheerful cries resound from outside the dwelling.

Ulima cuts through this with stern words, "But you'll work. No free meals in this tribe. Everyone has to pull their weight." The girls agree to this and Ulima's visage brightens, "Well then, you are welcome here, Drakoda."

Chapter 9

Elemental

The girl's time among the Cloudstalkers is well spent as there are many things to do despite the ever cooling weather. It turns out that there were several other hunting parties besides Lolani and Weiya stationed at key points along the feral herd's migration path in the Northern Plains. Only a few are still active, hunting ferals further west along the mountains. All have brought in their share of meats, hides, and other parts that require further work to be made into a wide variety of foods and goods that will be used by the Cloudstalkers or traded for things not readily available to them.

Already having some knowledge of the process, the girls are first tasked with drying foods. This includes not only meats but also nuts, berries, and vegetables found in the forest. They do this with many of the younger members of the tribe under the tutelage of a few adults. The girls discover that the zalonya tree produces a particularly large spherical nut that only grows in the winter. It's edible but its shell is incredibly durable. One of the adult Cloudstalkers demonstrates how heat makes the shell more flexible until it can be pierced with a sharp knife or talon, allowing access to the tasty seed within. These along with many other things brought in by gatherers are hung from rope, made from woven grass and leaves, to dry in the near constant mountain breeze.

Twinkaleni earns high praise for using her water siphoning spell to greatly increase the speed at which foods, especially meats, dry. The process of drying jerky enough to make pemmican usually takes a week or more, but Twinkaleni cuts it down to only a few minutes. The effort exhausts her though the Murin mage says it is well worth it to not only help improve their relations with the Ornivian tribe but get in some excellent practice. The girls help powder the now very dry meat using Zalonya seed pod shells as mortars and stone pestles. They mix various dried nuts, berries, and herbs in with the meat and add melted fat in to make a grayish goop. This is set aside to harden and stored for later consumption.

Another activity the girls learn along with the juvenile tribe members is scraping hides. Lolani and Weiya had shown them how to do this some in the plains but just enough to make them suitable for transport to the village, now they had to be cleaned thoroughly. This meant using a special rock, called a scraper, to rid the animals' skins of any remaining meat, fat, and membrane. This is a time consuming and tiring process, but the results of all their labors are beautiful hides that can then be made into warm clothing, blankets, pouches, flooring, and even traded as is.

When the scraper stones available become too dull to work with, the girls get to see how new ones are made. The Cloudstalkers have a unique way of fashioning their scrapers. This involved dropping a certain type of stone onto a rocky outcropping from very high up. Occasionally the stone will fracture into shards, sometimes yielding a piece with a straight and sharp enough edge that can then be made into a new scraper. It strikes Alice as a bit odd that they continued to use such seemingly primitive methods and tools when they could trade for Arsalian steel. She finds that they are perfectly aware of more advanced methods and technologies but prefer to teach their reliable traditions.

While work is laborious, it's never boring. The younger Cloudstalkers are very curious about the furred ones among them. Not many can speak the common tongue of Arsalia, generally only those tasked with hunting and trading bother to learn, but this doesn't stop them from using the few words they know to try to get the girls to reveal bits about themselves. In time and with the help of bilingual members, repetition, and many crude drawings in the dirt or on sheets of bark, Alice and her friends slowly pick up pieces of the Cloudstalker's language.

At first, everyone is eager to know about the Blood War raging far to the west along the borders of Arsalia and Feoria. They particularly want to know when it will end and when their mothers, fathers, brothers, and sisters will be returning to them. It seems to frustrate them that the girls don't know about the war their own people have caused but this is mostly due to the Ornivian's deep desire to have their families reunited. Once they understand that the girls have no news of the conflict, they ask more about them personally.

Alice, Danahlia, Twinkaleni, and Kaliska tell them stories of their adventures and how they came to be among them. The Cloudstalkers very much enjoy their tales and are always eager for more. Alice doesn't particularly like telling lengthy stories but Danahlia revels in the attention, often greatly embellishing the girl's deeds when she isn't entirely making them up, much to the feathered people's amusement.

The Cloudstalkers enjoy telling stories too, particularly at evening meals which are communal events. Elders will gather the younger members around for tales often laced with life lessons. One

Ulima tells has a chieftain who had just been happily wed. One day, the chieftain's young bride fell ill and died rather suddenly. Sure she was poisoned by his enemies, the chieftain waged a long and brutal campaign against his foes until, at great cost, they were defeated. As he stood atop the ruin of his rivals, he looked back to his own lands, to his own burned villages, and to his own heaps of bloody dead to find that his obsessions with hate and vengeance had done more damage to his people than his enemies ever had.

As time passes, the girls make a home for themselves in a large hollow nook at the base of an ancient Zalonya tree near the Cloudstalker's camp. From here they venture out and explore the mountains, or at least, Alice, Twinkaleni, and Kaliska do. Danahlia and Squiggles become increasingly lethargic as the winter brings snow and ever colder temperatures. The pair often prefer to stay home, curled together under feral skin blankets with a nice fire going. Twinkaleni says this is due to their cold blood, the low temperatures making it particularly difficult for them to keep warm and active so they take to sleeping much of the time. Fortunately, this also means Squiggles doesn't eat as much.

The other three venture out in their naturally thick winter coats and heavy, tribe made garments in search of various things. Firewood is always a welcome discovery. The Cloudstalkers do not cut down their beloved Zalonya trees, thus only fallen wood is allowed to be collected, even in the winter. A benefit of having such large trees around, however, is that when a decent sized branch is found fallen, it can usually supply the tribe for a good while. The girls also forage for various edible items as a surprising number of things are available to eat in the mountains if one knows where to look.

The trio finds that there are fresh water clams available in many of the Gadara Mountain's ponds and waterways. They aren't particularly large, but are plentiful as long as you're willing to brave the chilled waters. Steadily rarer patches of green also sometimes yield foods like wild onions and garlic, which go nicely in clam soup.

On one foraging trip, Weiya has led the girls to some smelly, steaming caves that can generally be expected to have edible mushrooms, among other things. They manage to find a few close to the entrance of one but not enough to have made the long walk worthwhile.

When Alice, Kaliska, and Twinkaleni try to go in further, the young Cloudstalker shrieks, "No! Not allowed to pass the sun, not allowed not allowed."

She points at the rough divide made from sunlight and the shadow of the cave's mouth.

"Why not?" asks Alice, "There might be more mushrooms deeper in."

"Not allowed. These are sacred caves. The mountain gods' children live in them. They let us take from here but no further. They'll get angry if we go in, they will they will," Weiya insists.

"The mountains have babies?" asks Kaliska, looking excitedly into the steam murky darkness.

Twinkaleni steps past the Chitali and calls forth a light to see by. When the bright, magical globe illuminates nothing but more rotten egg smelling steam billowing from further in, she sends it floating down ahead of her to reveal another patch of mushrooms.

Alice points them out, "There, see? There's a few more."

Weiya peers in but doesn't move.

"You can stay here, we'll get them and be right back," Alice assures her.

Weiya nods after a moment, "Be right back. Other caves there are, there are there are."

Alice agrees to this and the trio makes for the mushrooms.

As they approach them, Twinkaleni stops, "I feel something."

"What?" Alice asks.

"I'm not sure," replies the Murin mage, "It's almost like back in the emberstone cavern but... different."

She moves forward again breathing in through her nose deeply as if smelling something good. Alice sniffs but only picks up the smelly, musty scent of the damp cave.

"I feel it too," reveals Kaliska, "Like old things, dusty forgotten things. Think it's the mountain babies?"

Twinkaleni continues to inhale, giving her head a subtle shake, "I don't know."

The cave becomes rather narrow when they reach the patch of mushrooms and the warm steam coming from further in makes their fur feel damp. Twinkaleni holds the light, looking further in the cave, while Kaliska and Alice gather the soggy fungi. As they do, Alice picks up a distorted noise echoing from deep in the misty darkness beyond Twinkaleni's light.

"What was that?" she wonders.

Kaliska stands straight, leaving her partially filled basket on the ground, "Oh, maybe it's them. Can we go see?"

"Perhaps it would be worth taking a look, we've come all this way after all, "Twinkaleni reasons, "And I'm rather interested in seeing these 'mountain god' children."

Alice admits she is curious herself and they're about to go further when Weiya calls, "Come on come on come on!"

This prompts the girls to resume their mushroom picking, but as they're taking the last, they hear the sound again, like stone sliding against stone.

"What do you think that is?" asks Alice.

"Maybe it's the mountain babies playing. Oh, we have to go see," begs Kaliska.

"Perhaps just a quick look is an order," suggests Twinkaleni.

Alice nods her agreement but as they turn to further investigate, Weiya calls again, "No further! Said you'd be right back, you did you did you did!"

Alice holds out her index finger to the irritated Wakuwai and the girls venture further into the cave.

Even with Twinkaleni leading with her light, it's difficult to see through all the steam. Kaliska blows and waves at it futily. After a time, the Murin mage has had enough.

With one hand still holding up her light, she cocks the other at her hip before thrusting it forward with a shout of, "Vespis flomino!"

Cold air from outside rushes in from behind and past the girls in a powerful wave that shoves back the steam, giving them a clear view of the larger cavern they've entered. The light Twinkaleni holds falls on what at first glance just looks like more cave... but then it moves. Sliding nosily across the rough floor, a large, door sized chunk of rock is revealed to be the appendage of a giant monster made of stone.

"Whiskers," Twinkaleni breathes as the creature turns to them, her light revealing only a portion of it.

Something like an arm flows by in a blur of shadow as what, Alice guesses, is the giant's head rotates around to them. Frozen in surprise and fear, the young Tokala can only watch as the creature looks at them, though looks might be too strong a term. Its face is only just because of its position on what Alice suspects is its massive, mostly rectangular head. It has no eyes and only the vaguest creases to indicate facial features. The only sounds it makes are the grind and pop of rocks being powdered while it's cramped, cavern filling body shifts around in the dark beyond the light.

As the steam builds back up around it, the stone giant moves towards them.

"That's a big baby," comments Kaliska, staring wide eyed.

"Run!" Alice shouts, picking up the mesmerized Twinkaleni and dashing out the way they'd come.

Kaliska follows and their footsteps are chased by the growing sounds of rock being pulverized behind them just before a massive impact sends vibrations through the cave nearly taking the fleeing girls off their feet. Kaliska bounds ahead and snatches up her mushroom filled basket as they break for the sunlight. The trio bursts free into the cold open air and tumble into yielding snow.

Alice rolls off of Twinkaleni to see Weiya hovering over her, demanding, "What did you do?! What did you do?! What did you do?!"

Rather than responding, Alice sits up and looks to the cave entrance, relieved to see only steam emerging from it.

"Lying furbacks!" Weiya screeches down at them, "Cursed you may be now! Cursed cursed cursed!" The upset Cloudstalker then begins to fly back in the direction of the village, calling behind her, "I will not be cursed with you, not me, not me not me!"

As Alice watches her go, Twinkaleni pops up from the snow, shaking it free of her. "How marvelous!" she exclaims, strangely cheerful.

Kaliska flicks some snow from her ears, "That's not good, being cursed is *not* good."

"What was that thing in there?" asks Alice, standing and brushing snow from herself.

Twinkaleni grins widely at her, a rare thing to see on the little mage, "I believe *that* was an earth elemental."

On the long walk back to their hollow, Twinkaleni goes on in length, explaining what she knows of elementals and why she suspects it was there. From what the happily jabbering Murin says, elementals can be created when magic is present in an area for a very long time. In that time, the magic fuses with and takes on the characteristics of its surroundings. She goes on to say that the emberstones they'd found in the Great Horn were likely created in this way. She suspects that the lone mountain is probably a dormant volcano and that the ambient magic must have imprinted aspects of the local magma onto the rock it had fused with, giving the emberstones their characteristic glow and warmth. Elementals are the result of similar interactions between nature and magical energies over extended periods.

Twinkaleni prattles on, completely

unconcerned if her companions are following any of what she is saying or not, "During this time, the magic emulated what was around it, in this case stone and likely some sort of life forms that must live nearby, though that is entirely speculation as no one really knows the exact process of how elementals are formed. The ones found are often believed to be ancient. I wonder how long that one has been down there. There must be a source of tremendous magical energy within these mountains to have produced such a large elemental, perhaps even a rift!"

"A rift?" Alice asks.

"Of course!" Twinkaleni exclaims, "I must have told you of rifts at some point."

Alice shakes her head prompting the Murin to explain that rifts are formed by weaknesses in the barrier dividing their mortal world from Fayelindran, the world of magic and fae. When a point is sufficiently weakened a rift may form. These holes between worlds allow for the passage of energy and sometimes even entities. All the magic and mystical beings in the mortal world are believed to have originally come from Fayelindran through rifts. The Murin goes on to say that great sorcerers of the distant past have forged powerful empires atop significant rifts, letting the raw magical energy spewing forth enhance their powers to near godlike levels.

"If I could tap into such energies, I might be able to strike down the Order of Thermathrogi myself," the Murin concludes, seemingly more to herself than to the others.

"That kind o' power sounds dangerous, Twinkaleni," says Alice, not much liking this talk of people being as powerful as gods.

The little mage waves a negligent hand to her, "Of course there is significant risk involved, but the possibility makes the effort all the more worthwhile. We *must* return to that cave."

"What about the elemental?" asks Kaliska.

Twinkaleni rubs one of her ears between two tiny, pink fingers, "Mmm, indeed. An obstacle that will require some thought."

"Maybe we shouldn't go back," advises Alice, "Weiya was pretty upset about it, and if they think the caves are sacred, we might make the tribe angry."

And the Cloudstalkers were angry. Weiya had warned her elders of the trio knowingly trespassing into their mountain gods' caves, upsetting their children, and in so doing, possibly bringing down a god's wrath upon themselves. By the time the girls return to their hollow, a portion of the tribe is waiting for them. Ulima herself has been carried down, the elder no longer capable of flying on her own, to pass judgment on the trio's transgression.

The girls answer honestly about their trespassing in the cave despite Weiya's warning and Ulima nods somberly, "Then, to ensure my people remain free of any curse you have brought with you, you may no longer live among us."

Alice can feel Twinkaleni's argument coming before the mage even says anything and stops it, "No, Twinkaleni. You'll just make it worse for us if you attack their beliefs. We just need to let it go."

The Murin looks in surprise to the Tokala with her large amber eyes, but then nods and sags in shame with her friends.

Ulima adds more lightly, "But seein' as how you already don't really live among us, I just want your word that you won't be goin' into that cave again."

She gets it and Kaliska adds, "We won't, not even for all the mushrooms." The deer girl then offers her basket full to the tribe, lightening the mood.

The trio returns to their home finding Danahlia and Squiggles right where they left them, in a pile of hides curled atop one another.

"Ngh, close the door," Danahlia complains wearily, tucking a foot and bare loop of her tail back under her blankets.

Kaliska returns the skins used to keep out the cold, using the Wakuwai method of a few bone beads and loops like buttons to secure the door flap closed. Alice strips off her heavy, snow wet garments and crawls under the blankets of beast hides, mostly given to them, and snuggles in behind Danahlia partially atop one of Squiggle's hind legs.

Danahlia wiggles back into Alice's thick fur with an appreciative moan and Alice asks, "So what'd you do today?"

Without opening her eyes, Danahlia mumbles, "You're lookin' at it. You?"

"Well, *we* got kicked out of the village," informs Alice.

"What?" Danahlia exclaims, her emerald eyes popping open.

"Yeah, but we got to see an elemental mountain baby," says Kaliska, sitting with a sack of dried vegetables.

"What?" Danahlia exclaims again, more confused.

"If you'd have only let me explain, perhaps they would have been more reasonable. 'Education is the light that guides from the path of ignorance,'" Twinkaleni quotes from somewhere, tending to their small fire.

Alice, having endured the hostility that befell her when she openly began to question the gods after her parents had both perished despite all her pleading prayers to them in her youth, says with heated confidence, "No. People don't wanna hear the truth. They want to *hope* and *believe* in things, even if they don't make sense. Telling 'em that their mountain god's kids are actually mindless earth magic things would just make 'em angry."

Danahlia shimmies under her blankets until she's turned enough to look at Alice, "What're guys talkin' about?"

So the girls tell their story of what had happened on a trip that started out with the intent of gathering some mushrooms.

With the trio's banishment, they are no longer asked to work and learn with the Cloudstalkers, though they continue to preserve their relations the best they can through adhering to their rules and occasionally trading. Lolani continues to check on them, offering news and knowledge she feels might help, though Weiya largely avoids the girls now, possibly fearing an impending curse. This does however free the girls up to explore more of their new mountain residence.

They do fairly well hunting despite the winter season. The Cloudstalkers have difficulty doing so in their mountain home. They prefer open air to maneuver and long clear lines of sight to spot prey, which the dense, tall treed forest does not provide in abundance. From the ground, the girls have no such hindrances, and with Alice and Danahlia's ever increasing skill with the bow and Twinkaleni's magic, they do manage to bring down the occasional feral.

The girls find that the mountains' many cliffs are host to game in the form of ram like beasts Twinkaleni says her book called Ovigons. Four legged and thickly furred, these creatures have a habit of leaping up precarious cliffs with mystifying ease whenever they sense danger. When directly threatened, they press their backs into nooks and crevasses in the cliff side, thrusting forth imposing horns that curl around the sides of their heads before jutting forth like swords at an upward angle. The Cloudstalkers tend to leave these alone because the cliff side means they risk smashing against rocks during a dive and the horns of the beasts can keep even the feathered hunters' large talons at bay. The beasts' instincts work against them though when set upon by Alice and her friends, they're risky defensive positions leaving them vulnerable to arrows and magic.

The Ovigons' hides make excellent blankets, there meat is good while lean, and their horns can be fashioned into durable blades fairly easily. When not in immediate need themselves, the girls will often trade these to the Cloudstalkers, who prize them just as much and even earn the young hunters some respect.

On the infrequent days that the girls can lure Squiggles out of the hollow, they try to teach the dragon to fly. They do this most often with Twinkaleni's magic. Now in the relative seclusion of the mountains, they no longer have any fear of the mage's overt displays of power attracting unwanted attention. This allows her to use her gravity altering earth magic to lift the others into the air and float them around to simulate flight. Twinkaleni will have Alice, Kaliska, and, when they can get her out of bed, Danahlia, fly around as the dragon watches, enthusiastically flapping their arms to encourage Squiggles to imitate with his wings.

Over time, he manages a sort of glide that he likes to use to pounce long distance on ferals he finds. He flaps a little for this, but doesn't seem to see the value in actual flight yet. The Cloudstalkers, the younger ones in particular, like to watch but most tend to keep their distance. Sometimes, a few of them will fly beside Squiggles as he glides, encouraging him to greater and greater feats. Lolani offers the benefit of her experience, and the dragon begins to gain the confidence to climb trees and leap off to glide even greater distances. With this technique, he is better able to surprise the mountains' wild beasts, confusing them with a blast of fire before landing atop them to deliver a lethal bite.

Anything brought down by Squiggles is left to

him, as the beasts are generally too scorched and torn to be of much use to anyone anyway. Despite his increasing success at hunting, he does so so infrequently that he doesn't grow very much throughout the winter. His wings, however, become noticeably larger and stronger. The girls aren't sure if this is a natural growth pattern for Gullveigaryans or not but take any improvement to be a good sign.

As the winter season drags on, the girls find themselves needing to venture further and further into the mountains in search of food and firewood. Twinkaleni, also, has not given up her desire to return to the steamy, mushroom caves in search of the power that has animated the elemental within. She frequently tries to convince her companions of the potential in searching the caves further, suggesting that there may be more mushrooms or other edibles there. She also wishes to uncover the source of the steam, saying that this too may be of some use to them.

Alice had been shooting down the proposal for weeks, reasoning that violating their word would only anger the Cloudstalkers. But as supplies run thin, even she finds herself reconsidering, if only in her head. True, there were mushrooms they could gather, and there were other caves they hadn't checked. What were the chances that they had elementals too?

Wondering this during another of Twinkaleni's seemingly more reasonable rants on why they should go, Alice asks, "What about elementals? There could be more of 'em."

"I've thought long on this and I believe I have a solution," Twinkaleni grins to a napping Squiggles.

Chapter 10

Fury

Since elementals are animated by magic, Twinkaleni believes that an adequate amount of Squiggles' dragon fire will unravel the energies that bind it together, returning the earth composing the elemental's body to its original inanimate state. Though she admits this is only a theory.

"How much would be 'adequate?'" wonders Alice, stirring some very watered down pemmican stew over their small fire.

Danahlia sits by her side, leaning into her to share their warmth under several layers of skins. A snowstorm has kept them indoors for several days now and temperatures continue to drop as does their supply of wood and food.

From the comfort of Kaliska's lap and also wrapped heavily in skins, Twinkaleni admits, "That is difficult to estimate. But, the confined space in which we are likely to encounter elementals, if we even do, should help focus any blast, thus reducing Squiggles' necessary effort."

"Think you can pull that off, Squigs?" Danahlia

calls back to Squiggles, who hasn't moved much since the storm began.

The dragon offers a snort from under the rest of their hide blankets though Alice isn't even sure he's awake.

While the storm lingers, the girls discuss plans and what they hope to find in the caves, if only to keep their minds off their dwindling supplies. By the time the storm is finally over, the idea has been passed around so much that the party has agreed to explore the caves once more. Danahlia and Squiggles come this time, eager to rid themselves of cabin fever's uncomfortable touch.

Squiggles leads the way, bursting through the snow that had built up over the slim entrance to their home between two massive surface roots, uncharacteristically excited to be out in the open, if still very cold, air. Looking up to the Cloudstalker's treehouses, they can see much of the tribe is busy ridding their village of snow and carefully removing any precariously hanging icicles that have formed on higher branches. The girls use this as an opportunity to head out while gathering as little attention as possible.

The party travels east toward a known pond,

not wanting any observant Cloudstalkers to get suspicious of them, before heading in a more northerly direction. Kaliska plucks pine needles as they walk, munching on them as they make guesses as to what else might be hidden in the steam of the caves. Twinkaleni has suggested that since there is steam at all, there must be some sort of heated water source, indicating that there may be a thermal vent within the mountains. This brings up fond ideas of bathing in hot water, something they've heard only the wealthy are reputed to do. Discussion of discovering natural or mystical heat sources within the caves help keep the girls invigorated as they trudge through the deep snow.

"It *must* be nice if rich people do it," Alice is saying when Squiggles suddenly sounds in surprise.

They all look to him whip around his head, something wrapped around his neck.

Just as Danahlia is asking, "Hey, what's that?" Another thin rope like thing coils around the dragon's throat.

It has a long tail that Alice follows back to the trees and to a near entirely white furred Lobovan man holding the end of the tail in his hands. He isn't alone. The girls find themselves quickly surrounded by a dozen or more people of varying species. As they appear from behind trees, they charge, hooting excitedly toward the girls while tossing more ropes over the angry dragon.

As Squiggles roars his outrage and snaps a few of the lines, Alice shouts, "Hey! Stop! What're you doing?!"

Her friends cry similar protests but the encroaching strangers pay them little mind. Alice sees some carrying clubs and knives, so she pulls her bow off her shoulder and nervously knocks an arrow.

"Bandits!" warns Twinkaleni.

"They're tryin' to take Squigs!" calls Danahlia, raising her spear to them.

A loose ring of male adult Warm Bloods forms and slows in its advance as the terrified girls prepare for a fight. The few trying to hold Squiggles as he squirms are forced closer by his thrashing and one only narrowly avoids a slash from Danahlia's spear.

A grinning Didel brandishing a knife confronts her, "Hey smoothie, think you know how ta-" before he can finish, Danahlia makes a lightning swift lunge, her spear point easily slipping in and out of the man's throat. He steps back, eyes wide in surprise, his knife falling to the now crimson snow at his feet. The man drops to his knees as others replace him, shouting angry racial obscenities.

Seeing this triggers the reality of the situation in Alice and she fires her arrow at the wolf man holding the rope around Squiggles' neck.

He sees it coming and narrowly avoids it, shouting, "Get the Tok, she's got a bow!"

As the other men shout warnings to their companions, Squiggles snaps at one that gets too close, ripping off a hand and then spitting it back with a blast of fire at another, causing panicked screams as the man is set ablaze.

Even over these, a thunderous roar resonates over all, "Get more bolas on that damned dragon! NOW!"

The voice is close and fearsome enough to demand Alice's attention. As she pans toward it, she sees Twinkaleni is already lying face down in the snow and is swiftly joined by Danahlia. Kaliska, unarmed and frozen with fear, is largely ignored as most are preoccupied with entangling Squiggles. A

Feladine has managed to leap up and grab onto Squiggles' muzzle, holding his mouth closed as more ropes are thrown over his limbs, neck, and tail, immediately becoming taut around him. A mountainous, black furred Urock tackles Squiggles, using his prodigious strength and size to knock the young dragon onto his side, pinning him down. Those free turn their attention to Alice with menacing smiles. Alice shouts for Kaliska to flee as she draws her sword, but before she can free her blade, she's struck hard over the head from behind. She feels cold then and as her vision fades to black, she sees Kaliska bounding for the trees with two men in hot pursuit.

Alice is brought back to aching awareness when Squiggles cries in pain and men shout.

The deep voice of the Urock booms angrily over them, "IDIOTS! We need it alive!"

The Tokala's heavy eyes open, revealing that she's floating a foot or so over the snow before the pain in her head lures her back into the comforting darkness.

A sudden chill over all of her body forces Alice conscious. She gasps awake to find her muzzle in the snow. Instinctively, she tries to lift herself from it with her hands but finds she can't bring them from behind her back, the strain in her wrists telling her they'd been tied together, as are her ankles. She hears excited unfamiliar male voices all around her and wiggles her body in an effort to roll over just as a foot shoves her roughly from one side, forcing her to it. A smiling Lobovan man, the same one she had tried to hit with an arrow, looks down at her, lit only by fire light. He suddenly drops to a crouch over her, causing Alice to flinch and his smile to widen.

"Mm-mm-mm, you *are* a pretty one," he says, looking over her hungrily. Alice finds she is no longer wearing her heavier winter garments and is left only with a badly torn shirt and shredded pants. She shrinks into herself, crossing her legs the best she can, her skin crawling, very conscious of the man's gaze.

A thin, brown and black patched Houdain approaches, asking, "What do we have 'ere," in a wheezy, more annoying than intimidating baritone.

The Lobovan puts a large hand on the smaller man's face and gives him an uninterested shove, hard enough to toss the dog man on his back, saying loudly but not taking his eyes off Alice, "I get this one first."

A few irritated but unchallenging comments are heard as the Houdain retreats. Alice is entirely focused on the wolf man standing over her, his hand approaching her face. Alice presses her head back into the snow, bearing her teeth at him, but he only smiles. When his fingers are inches away, she snaps at him, catching two of his fingers between her canines. She bites down as hard as she can but the man just keeps smiling, though now more menacingly. Alice tastes the man's blood and keeps on the pressure until his other hand strikes her so hard across the cheek, she spits his fingers free with a pained yip. Forced to look over, her vision blurry, she sees a still unconscious Twinkaleni. Past her, Danahlia is in the snow, squirming furiously within a gathering of other men, her limbs tied and a rope around her muzzle.

They grab at her, pulling on her tail and squeezing her chest through what's left of her clothes. Now that Alice devotes what little focus she can manage to it, she can hear their ugly comments.

"I always wondered if these egger girls were as smooth on the inside as they are on the outside," one standing over her growls.

A Mustaroni squeezes the Liguna's bare thigh, "Got some meat on her too. Bet she's nice and warm."

Another, mostly obscured by the other two, runs a hand over Danahlia's neck, "I'll take that. I 'ear these puddle hopers 'r' cold as they blood."

"Only one way ta find out," grumbles the massive black Urock, lumbering into view from where Alice can just make out Squiggles on the other side of the fire, every inch of him tied up and weighed down with large stones.

One of the men complains, "Oh come on, you're gonna ruin 'er. At least let us have a go first."

The giant bear man merely thrusts his head toward the complainer who immediately shrinks away as the others groan over their poor luck. The Urock kneels down and rips off what's left of Danahlia's clothes with a negligent swipe of his clawed paw, exposing the Lizard girl's body to the snow. He then drops to his knees, blocking the Liguna from view, tossing the rope that was binding her ankles over his shoulder while commanding two other men, eagerly watching nearby, to hold her legs open.

From the corner of her eye, Alice sees movement and looks back to see the white furred wolf man looming over her, his nose just over her own with sharp teeth bared, "Best keep it here, Missy. You got your own problems."

He then rips her already tattered shirt free of her shivering form. He looks at her naked chest admiringly before dropping atop her. Feeling this stranger's heavy, warm weight over her exposed body makes Alice shriek in panic. Expecting horrible things to happen, Alice closes her eyes tight, holds a breath, and waits for it to end. But the man doesn't move.

Thinking there would be far more pain and motion involved, Alice looks down at the man's face in her chest. She shivers under him only to find his entire body slack. Alice looks around as another, the unimpressive Houdain, takes notice and approaches. The dog man looks at the Lobovan curiously just before his eyes go wide. He then collapses in an awkward heap. Not understanding, Alice looks around, frightened, to find Twinkaleni awake beside her. She hadn't risen, tied up herself, but her eyes glow with the unnatural gold light Alice had seen only a few times before.

The Houdain fell close enough to the fire that a pant leg catches and alerts a few others. Most are too busy cheering the Urock with Danahlia to pay much mind, but shocked cries and unsettling odors begin to get their attention.

The Urock is in the middle of lowering his trousers when he looks angrily over and shouts "Morons! Put that ou-" The bear man freezes mid thought as Twinkaleni turns her furious gaze towards him.

An alarmingly haunting sound, like a howling wind given voice, blows in from everywhere and nowhere, "GET, AWAY, FROM HER!"

The startled men look around, alert, some scrambling for weapons. The Houdain's coat catches readily, adding a growing hellish light to the scene as men look around into the pitch black night under the forest canopy.

The massive Urock starts to tip over. With her legs free, Danahlia braces the man's incredible weight to the side so she isn't crushed.

One of the men who was holding Danahlia's ankles, now standing, gives the Urock a few light kicks, "Breck? Breck?!"

The bear man doesn't move.

"GET AWAY FROM HER!" the voice shrieks like a banshee through the camp once more, making Alice wish her hands were free so she could cover her ears.

"Look! The little one!" the Feladine says, pointing from where he sits atop Squiggles.

"A witch!" someone cries, "Get 'er quick!"

Alice squirms as the bandits mobilize but she can't get a hand or even a foot free of her bindings.

Breathing raggedly, Twinkaleni looks to the camp fire and the burning Houdain, screaming, "Feasta!"

The flames leap forth, splashing over two men and onto Squiggles. The Feladine manages to roll over the dragon, using the bound reptile's body as a shield to hide from the inferno. Danahlia struggles to a crouch and springs feet first into the weasel man heading toward Twinkaleni with a knife. He ends up tumbling through the campfire and over the Houdain, catching himself. As he screams and rolls in the snow, Alice spots a man past him with her bow, an arrow pointing at the enraged mage.

As her eyes fall on the point of one of her own

arrows, it flies forth. Before Alice can even finish shouting her name, the arrow pierces the Murin high in the chest. Instantly the glow in the small girl's eyes goes out as her head falls back to the snow, turning slackly to the side.

Alice screams, "No!" as Danahlia rolls on the ground, desperately avoiding a man trying to chop down at the lizard girl's head with Alice's sword. He misses once, but on the second swing, Danahlia can't move her tail out of the way and he cleaves it off, leaving the separated appendage wiggling wildly in the snow. Danahlia's pained cry is muffled by the rope keeping her mouth shut and as the man raises Jellybane again, she only looks up at him in teary eyed horror.

"STOP!" Alice shrieks from under the Lobovan, and the man with her sword stills. Not because of Alice, but because of a piercing hawk's cry from above.

From the night, large black talons glimmer in the firelight as they grab hold of the man's head, piercing eyes and tearing flesh. The man cries out, dropping Jellybane to grasp his ravaged face. Lolani beats her powerful wings and disappears back into the darkness as more ear splitting screeches sound.

More talons reach down for the panicked men, tearing ears, stabbing eyes, and shredding muzzles as they scream, fleeing for their lives. They don't get them. Some of the smaller men are taken from their feet and sent tumbling into rocks and trees with crushing force, while others are left blinded and crippled by talons only to be ended by the run of bone bladed knives across their throats.

The fire Twinkaleni had bathed Squiggles in, burns through enough of the ropes holding the dragon, so he too can join the fray. He immediately targets the running Feladine man and leaps for him, using his wings to carry him over and then atop the cat man. Squiggles doesn't kill him immediately, but instead holds him down before roasting him with his fiery breath, roaring his rage as he does.

Seeing the battle winding down, Alice wiggles from under the dead wolf man over to Twinkaleni's prone form and places her head on her chest, warm tears running down her face. Her eyes flash open, she hears a heartbeat. Kaliska appears, near breathless.

The Chitali falls to her knees in the snow, "Oh geeze, oh geeze oh geeze oh geeze."

"Kali!" Alice exclaims.

Kaliska looks to Alice worriedly, "Yeah?"

"You're alive?" is all Alice can muster through her shivering and tears.

Kaliska's mouth hangs open as she nods. "Yeah. I got, uh, them," she says, looking around at the handful of Cloudstalkers landing all around to finish what's left of the bandits. She then refocuses on the arrow stuck in Twinkaleni, "Oh geeze, oh geeze. Do I take it out or do I leave it in? Do I take it out or do I leave it in?"

"She's still alive, you have to help her," pleads Alice.

Kaliska nods for a few moments before saying, "Ok," she then takes in a deep breath, "Ok, ok." The deer girl places a hand on the Murin's chest and gives the arrow a swift tug. The arrow comes free, bloodless. Kaliska feels around in surprise, then says, "It didn't go through."

A Cloudstalker kicks the Lobovan off her legs and cuts through Alice's bindings, letting her check on the mage herself. Twinkaleni had been the only one not stripped of her heavy garments and the brittle, merely wooden tip of the arrow hadn't had the power to pierce the many layers of hides she wore, though it had come close before the point snapped, blunting the missile.

"She ok?" asks Danahlia, teeth chatter and body shivering as she comes to stand over them.

"Danny!" Alice cries, standing to hug the nude and very cold girl.

"I think so, just used too much magic," says Kaliska.

"Good. Think you can do somethin' about this?" Danahlia asks, turning to show the large open wound left by the loss of nearly three quarters of her tail. It wasn't bleeding nearly as much as such a wound would warrant.

Alice kneels to examine it, her heart pained at the sight, "Oh, your tail. Does it hurt?"

Danahlia swiftly shifts her hips to get it away from Alice's probing fingers, "Yes! It does."

As Kaliska heals Danahlia, Lolani pulls Alice's heavy winter coat off a dead man and put's it over the shivering Tokala.

Alice sniffs, the adrenaline leaving her body making her feel terribly weak, "Thank you." She can't help herself and falls into Lolani's chest repeating her words over and over as tears dampen the woman's feathers. Lolani says nothing, just wraps her wings around the fox girl.

After her wound is sealed, Danahlia is given back her winter garments as well and takes Lolani's place around Alice. Then Kaliska joins in, followed by Squiggles.

As the girls try to settle themselves after the ordeal, they watch as the Cloudstalkers comb over the bandits, taking weapons, clothes, and anything else they might find useful. They even go so far as to bash in some of the dead men's faces with the rounded pommels of their knives. At first, Alice thinks this is out of anger or some form of revenge, but soon finds they're actually taking trophies in the form of the bandit's teeth, favoring larger canines. She would see these again on the tribal warriors, hanging prominently displayed from necklaces and braids, with some of the more experienced among them possessing an impressively macabre collection.

The Cloudstalkers escort the girls home, some flying ahead to be sure the path is clear, while Lolani and two others stay with them. Lolani tells them that they had been aware of the mountain bandits for some time, though the fiends rarely came this far east. She surmises that Squiggles is likely why they had risked entering the Cloudstalker's territory, commenting that furred ones have always had a deep desire to claim the power of dragons.

Once back in the safety of their home, the tribe reopens to the girls. After such misfortune, they are confident that any curse has been shed and celebrate the fall of their enemies. Weiya admits she was following the girls when the ambush happened and met up with Kaliska after the Chitali had lost her pursuers. The hawk girl then went to tell the rest of the tribe. Though Weiya was forbidden from joining the attack, she assures the girls that she had saved them yet again. The girls decide they've had enough exploring for now and remain close to the hollow and their Wakuwai friends.

Many weeks pass before winter finally begins to break. The high mountain snows start to melt, causing trickling streams to steadily swell into rivers while turning modest ponds into lakes. With the warming weather, green thrusts forth from once bare frozen earth and ferals reemerge from their winter dens to eat it. Danahlia's tail has begun to grow back, a grayish finger thick nub poking out of what's left of the once lengthy appendage. She can even move it a little.

The Cloudstalkers celebrate the coming spring by feasting on anything and everything left over in their stores, which, with all their preparations for winter, is enough for several days of careless consumption. The girls are invited to celebrate with them and Squiggles is often at the center of many cheers and songs as the young dragon has, at long last, begun to fly. He much prefers starting off from a high point rather than taking off from the ground, but now flaps his wings with enthusiasm along with the Ornivians who jubilantly fly around him. He likes the attention, and especially the treats they toss him, encouraging his efforts to stay aloft for longer and longer periods.

The celebrations have an unfortunate purpose however. The Cloudstalkers will soon be leaving their winter camp and making the long journey to their summer site, far to the east along the coast of the Azuma Sea. They wouldn't have the carrying capacity to bring large stores of food along with their belongings, so they eat all they can now to have the energy to make the arduous flight. Despite the journey likely taking months on foot, the girls are assured that they would be welcomed and even that the sea would provide an abundance of fish during their stay. The girls politely decline the offer, intending to remain in the greening mountains they had taken so long to reach.

As the weather warms and the last of the celebrations are had, the girls bid the Cloudstalkers a very fond farewell. Lolani is the last to leave, assuring them that the tribe will return in the fall for the herds' annual migration.

With that, she takes flight after her kin and calls back, "Clear skies, Drakoda!" before disappearing past the trees.

Alice sighs, looking up at the now empty, silent homes of their feathered friends, already missing their presence. Danahlia places a comforting hand on her shoulder as Kaliska continues to wave after the tribe even though they are no longer visible.

Twinkaleni claps her tiny hands together, "Well, no time like the present. Let us make preparations at once."

"Preparations for what?" Danahlia asks.

"Now that there will be no objection, this is the perfect opportunity to explore those caves," claims Twinkaleni, "Come along, mystery, discovery, and knowledge await!" The Murin mage walks purposely toward their hollow.

"Welp, I haven't seen that elemental thing yet," says Danahlia, following.

"Maybe we can make friends with it, wouldn't that be fun?" bubbles Kaliska, bouncing after the pair.

Alice grins and looks to Squiggles, "Come on boy, let's go have us an adventure."

Epilogue

The girls travel to the caves, remaining alert after their encounter with the bandits. Aside from a hungry bear that Squiggles quickly dispatches with his growing strength, nothing impedes them this time. When they reach the unpleasantly smelling steam caves, they search around until discovering one large enough for their dragon to fit through. Squiggles eagerly enters the cave, sniffing and scratching at the walls with his powerful claws. Occasionally, he'll break loose a bit of steam damp rock to taste, which only seems to interest him in exploring further.

They find more mushrooms hidden in the steam and add them to their stores. They've packed well for this expedition. Having planned on staying by the caves for at least a few days, the girls have loaded themselves, as well as Squiggles, with supplies. While they explore the depths of the steam warm labyrinth, they discover these tunnels are host to various insects, ranging from small skittering beetles to some very large worms. The beetles can frequently be found in clusters eating mushrooms. The worms, however, are often in tunnels they appear to dig themselves. These grub like creatures have frightening eyeless visages equipped with multiple sets of fearsome mandibles surrounding ever open maws filled with crushing teeth set in strange, spiraling rings. Fortunately, the monstrous cave dwellers are particularly slow and only show interest in digging their tunnels or undulating through larger ones. It becomes suspected that even larger versions of these creatures may very well have dug the steam caves the girl's now travel in, an unsettling thought.

A benefit to encountering these insects is that the party doesn't fear running short of food. A quick fire blast from Squiggles has the cave smelling even more terrible, but yields roasted insects along with sometimes only slightly scorched mushrooms. The insects aren't particularly well liked, as they taste very much like dirt, but Squiggles happily dines on them while the girls stick to their stores. During their day or so long venture through the darkness, lit predominately by Twinkaleni's magic, they do not encounter any elementals but the occasional deep rumbling in the earth is a reminder that they are there, somewhere in the steamy depths of the mountains.

The tunnel they follow twists and turns, even branching off in different directions, including upward, but the girls don't have any fear of losing their way. Squiggles frequently claws at the stone and once even has to dig through a particularly narrow area, leaving his unique marks along their path. Still, they are glad to finally see light at the end and cheer, racing to it.

As the girls and their dragon burst free upon a wide cliff on the other side of the Gadara mountain range, they bask in the warm sunlight, letting it take the steam's damp from their fur and skin while breathing deep the sweet smelling air. Beyond them lies the unexplored Wildlands, a dense forest that extends all the way to the horizon with only a single, distant, spire of a mountain to break the vast expanse of green.

They're alone on the rocky cliff, save for a few hardy shrubs, and make their way to the edge. Just high enough to see over the tallest trees, Alice sits to rest, admiring the glorious vista bathed in a new day's sun. She's quickly joined by Danahlia and Kaliska, expressing their relief to finally be free of the cave. Twinkaleni, however, remains standing, silently shielding her eyes as she peers to the horizon.

Kaliska tugs one of the mouse girl's sleeves and then pats her lap invitingly but the small mage remains vigilant. Alice follows the Murin's intense gaze to the thin mountain and notices it has tipped slightly, its narrow peak no longer pointing straight to the sky.

Thinking it must be crumbling, Alice points, "Look, that mountain's fallin' down."

A slight rumble reverberates through the earth seemingly to confirm this. Though as they watch in anticipation, the mountain's peak slowly straightens, the entire thing just a smidge to the west from where it was. Thinking this very odd, the girls continue to watch as it does this several more times, each time sending rumbles through the ground, felt even so far away.

"It's not falling... it's moving," says Kaliska in awe as Alice's mouth steadily drops open.

"Oh ticks," Danahlia whispers nervously.

"It cannot be..." Twinkaleni breathes, "... a titan."

About the Author:

K.J. Bailey (Kenichiro Justin Bailey) has thus far only written the Alice Dippleblack series, but looks forward to creating more fantastical worlds.

www.ingramcontent.com/pod-product-compliance
Lightning Source LLC
Chambersburg PA
CBHW020558180626
46810CB00007B/2555